Pepperland

Pepperland

Mark Delaney

PEACHTREE
ATLANTA

Published by
PEACHTREE PUBLISHERS
1700 Chattahoochee Avenue
Atlanta, Georgia 30318-2112

www.peachtree-online.com

Text © 2004 by Mark Delaney
Cover illustration © 2004 by Richard C. Keep

Cover design by Loraine Joyner
Book design by Melanie McMahon Ives

Manufactured in the United States of America
10 9 8 7 6 5 4 3 2 1
First Edition

ISBN 1-56145-317-X

Library of Congress Cataloging-in-Publication Data

Delaney, Mark.
  Pepperland / written by Mark Delaney.-- 1st ed.
    p. cm.
  Summary: Struggling to come to terms with the death of her mother in 1980, sixteen-year-old Beatles fan Star Cochran hopes to find closure by delivering to John Lennon a letter her mother wrote to him in 1964 but never sent.
  ISBN 1-56145-317-X
  [1. Mothers and daughters--Fiction. 2. Grief--Fiction. 3. Beatles--Fiction. 4. Lennon, John, 1940-1980--Fiction. 5. Guitar--Fiction.] I. Title.

PZ7.D373185Pe 2004
[Fic]--dc22
                                        2004005435

*Of course,
this is for Roberta Delaney,
my mother,
who is, was, and always will be with me*

Special thanks
to

John LeVan
of LeVan's Guitar Repair in Nashville, Tennessee,
the best luthier around
(and the only repairman who touches my guitars!),
for kindly making sure Teri Seegar knew what she was doing

and

Douglas A. Mays, Ph.D.,
Psychologist for the Hickman County, Tennessee, School System,
for keeping a professional eye on Dr. Artaud.

If there's a mistake in these pages, don't blame these guys!

Contents

1

Things We Said Today

I told the shrink that my mother named me Pamela Jean because she had to.

Mom always loved the Beatles. When she was just seventeen, she swiped a dollar from her boyfriend's jacket and used it to buy a 45 rpm single of "I Want to Hold Your Hand" and "I Saw Her Standing There." From that instant the Fab Four were her life. She loved the chiming harmonies in *Meet the Beatles!*, the sadness in *Beatles '65*, the freaky experimentation in *Rubber Soul* and *Revolver*. I have vague memories of dancing with her to *Sgt. Pepper's Lonely Hearts Club Band*, even though I was only three when the album hit the stores. Later she told me that in 1970, when she first heard the *Let it Be* album, she cried because she knew it was the end. She never said the end of what, but I understood she meant more than just the breakup of a band.

When she was pregnant with me, Mom would play Beatles records stacked five high on a plastic phonograph, and she would feel me roll and kick, almost always in time to the music. Mom loved the music and that whole sixties thing. She wanted to name me Star or River or Moonbeam, one of those corny names that went out of style with lava lamps and sitar music. Her parents threw a fit, though, and Mom relented. She

named me Pamela after her mother and Jean after her father—
whose name is Eugene.

Now, for the record, my name is Star. Only Star.

The shrink's name is Dr. Leslie Artaud. Two months ago,
when I first saw her name stenciled on the door to her office,
I thought it was pronounced Ahr-TODD. I got it wrong three
or four times before she finally corrected me. She said it was
Ahr-TOH. She even swept up her pinky to chalk that little
accent mark over the second syllable. Ahr-*TOH*. She says the
French pronunciation is a little unusual, and that it's okay if I call
her Leslie. I don't. It seems phony, and I don't need a big sister.

I'm sitting on the floor of her office. The first day we met
she said I should make myself comfortable, so I went straight
to the floor and crossed my legs. That little move made her
eyebrow shoot up, but she didn't say anything. Now I sit on
the floor every time we meet—each Thursday from 4:00 to
4:50—while Dr. Ahr-*TOH* and I have our little chats.

Today I have my electric guitar with me. I hold it in my lap,
and my head tilts down as I stare at the fingerboard. Angling
my head this way makes my hair fall across my face so that it
covers one eye completely and forms a sort of veil over the
other. Through it I can just see Dr. Artaud sitting in her leather
office chair. She swivels slowly back and forth, placing the
eraser end of a pencil against her chin and twirling it as she
studies me. She's not happy. She knows I don't have to look at
my fingers when I play. I can close my eyes, or look at the person sitting across from me, or even lean over and take a sip of
Coke from a straw without so much as letting a finger slip.
She's already figured that I'm staring down and letting my
hair cover me because it's the only way I can be alone between
4:00 and 4:50 on a Thursday afternoon.

"Pamela," she says. "Pamela Jean?" I move my head to the
music I'm playing, making a show out of refusing to answer.

Dr. Artaud stops swiveling and sets the pencil down. "Very well. Star?"

My head comes up. I'm in the middle of a blues riff, something I picked up off of one of Syke's Clapton records, and I want to let it finish. My fingers form a minor diminished chord and let it travel from the fifth fret down to the first, finally resolving into an E major. Without an amplifier, the strings on the electric sound tinny, as though I'm strumming loose wires.

"Nice," Dr. Artaud says. She takes this very deep breath before speaking again, and already I'm on guard. If she needs this much time to choose her words, it's a fair guess I'm going to hate what she's about to say. I run my fingers through my hair, combing it back so she can see that I'm ready for it, that I'm looking her in the eye.

"Star," she begins, "when I gave you permission to bring the guitar to our session, it was with the understanding that you were not going to use it to avoid the issues we need to work on. Remember?"

I love the words she chooses. I'm sixteen, my mom died three months ago, and that's an *issue?* I have news for her. What I'm going to wear to school tomorrow is an issue. Whether or not to change the strings on my guitar is an issue.

"Now, don't misunderstand," she continues. She's using that tone I hate—that steady, walking-on-eggs tone that says she's worried my head might explode if she says the wrong thing. "I believe your interest in music is healthy. But as with anything else, you should perhaps consider a little moderation." She pauses. "I'm thinking specifically of your academic performance. Your father tells me you're failing your classes."

My head drops again, and my fingers slip into some power chords. If I were plugged in, the walls would be vibrating.

"*Star,*" she says, a little sharply. It's as much anger as I've ever seen from her. Dr. Artaud is a smallish woman, with tight auburn curls cut close to her head and a noticeable hunch in her shoulders. She usually speaks very quietly, her hand drawing slow circles in the air while she conjures up the words she wants. This raising of the voice is out of character, and it catches my attention. My fingers wrap around the guitar's neck, muting the strings. "Is that true?" she asks. "Are you failing your classes?"

Clearly there's no ducking the question, so I slip the leather strap from around my neck and lay the guitar back into the open case. I slap down the latches and look up at Dr. Artaud. "Yeah," I say. "Yeah, I guess I am."

"Are you going to tutoring, as we agreed?"

I start to say yes, figuring it's not exactly a lie, but it's the "as we agreed" part that catches me. I'm supposed to go to tutoring twice a week. I've gone maybe three times in the last month. Hidden behind my knee, the fingers of my left hand stretch and play silently, searching for a guitar I'm no longer holding.

"I see," says Dr. Artaud. I hear nothing accusatory or judgmental in the way she says it, but the words still rankle. She joins her hands together, fingertips touching, and raises them to her mouth. This is another one of her many thinking gestures, just like the screwing-the-pencil-into-the-chin trick. She nods to herself, and the hands bob up and down with the motion of her head. "Star," she finally says, "I know your music means a lot to you." She's drawing the circles now, consulting her notes as she does, and I sense we're about to revisit old territory. "We've discussed this on a number of occasions, but have you considered writing a song for your mother?"

I'm glad I'm sitting when she says it. I feel my knees turn to water. I look away from her, and my hands feel sweaty. I rub my palms back and forth against the legs of my jeans, again and again, until they warm from the friction.

"Star?"

"No," I say. "I mean, I'm not sure I'm there yet."

She nods, pretending to have a clue. "You might want to look at it another way, Star. You're saying that writing a song for your mother is something that can only happen after you've worked through all the grief and anger. In a sense, the song is a kind of destination. I'm suggesting the reverse, that you might write a song as a *means* of getting there. It doesn't have to be the destination; it can be the path."

I say nothing. I've tried countless times to write a song for my mother. When I was four or five, Mom would bring me to the park, and I would chase after the flock of pigeons that gathered around the picnic area. They'd take off in what seemed like a million different directions, this rustling, gray-black cloud, with me running after them, my fingers outstretched and my hands empty. That's what happens when I try to write a song about my mother. My thoughts scatter. My fingers can't find the guitar strings. My hands are empty.

"I'll think about it," I tell the doctor. And I will. I really will.

"That's all I'm asking." She looks at me then as if she's expecting me to say more. I think she's thinking that something terribly important has just passed between us, like maybe we've reached some sort of breakthrough moment or something. If so, I've missed it. When she finally realizes I have nothing more to say, she seems disappointed. She glances at a tiny gold watch on her wrist. "I guess that's all for today then," she says. "I'll see you again next week."

I scoop up my guitar case and hug it against me as I leave.

☆

Pepperland

John Lennon wrote a couple of songs about his mother. The first was called "Julia." That was his mother's name—Julia. My mother's name was Catherine. She was taller than me, and prettier I think, and she had a bit of an Irish rhythm in her voice that she got from her grandfather. Julia died when Lennon was seventeen years old. She stepped into the street and was run over by a drunk driver. My mom died of breast cancer. In a way, I guess I'm luckier than John Lennon was. He was raised mostly by his aunt Mimi and didn't really get to know Julia until just a few short months before she died. I had my mom for sixteen years, so, as I said, I guess luck is sort of relative.

I'm making a mental note: Lennon wrote another song for Julia. It came later, long after the Beatles broke up. I wish now that I could remember the name of it.

The case that holds my guitar is great. It's ancient—leather wrapped over solid wood. I could drop the whole thing, guitar included, down a flight of stairs and not have to worry about dinging my ax. The downside, though, is that my particular ax, a vintage 1952 Fender Telecaster, happens to weigh a ton as electric guitars go, so handling all the weight can be a real pain. It sometimes feels like my right arm is two inches longer than my left, stretched out like an old piece of elastic from carrying the guitar for so long.

I set the case down on the floor and wait for the elevator doors to swish open. The receptionist in Dr. Artaud's building waggles a finger at me to say good-bye, but I pretend not to see it. I'm not in the mood to chat about nail polish, and that seems to be her favorite subject. Besides, I clip my fingernails down to the quick—better for guitar playing—so

I'm not really interested in having hands that look like they belong on the cover of *Seventeen.*

By the time I make it halfway through the parking lot, the muscles in my arm are cramping. I shift the case from my right hand to my left and wait for those muscles to complain. The medical building behind me is a glassy black tower, and the sun hitting it reflects into golden ripples on the blacktop in front of me. A hundred yards ahead is the highway, the cars little more than a shifting blur of colors. Their engines make a vague, general hum that keens upward as they approach and then bends down, like a blues note, as they speed away. I like the sound and file it away in my head. Can I do that in a song? Can my fingers find it on the guitar neck? Maybe—or maybe that sound is like everything else that catches you by surprise and makes you smile. You hold onto it, you struggle to recreate it, but you can't make it work.

I'll try it, I tell myself. And just to make sure I'm listening, I think it again: *I'll try it.*

At the corner is a wood-slat bench with sides and legs of black iron. Surrounding it is a huge, boxy rain shelter made of some kind of amber plastic. My bus stop. I set the guitar down, sit, and wait. Slipped in a frame to my right is a movie poster—Robert De Niro, with sweaty face and blackened eyes, staring at me. Below the image, red block letters scream the title, *Raging Bull.*

Syke's leather jacket is way too big for me, but I like it that way. I roll the sleeves and tug the collar up around my neck.

☆

My favorite stretch of beach is only twenty minutes from the shrink's office, and I take the bus there after every session. I hate the beach on a summer morning, when the bodies are lined up on the sand like hot dogs on an outdoor grill, but I love it on a fall evening. The day is cool, the sun is low in the sky, and sometimes I'm the only one here. I smile when the bus doors hiss open and I see only three cars in the parking lot. The sun is huge, a giant orange fireball hanging just above the horizon, and little trails of light wiggle off of it. The trails of light are reflections on the surface of the water. I just stand there a moment, taking it all in. I'm maybe 200 yards from where the breakers are washing against the sand, and the water is roaring in my ears. The sound is all around me. Sometimes I think I can taste it in the air—the sound, I mean—but then I figure I'm just getting all romantic about salt spray.

My mother used to bring me here. Before I was old enough to go to school, she would pack lunch in one of those old-fashioned wicker baskets: peanut butter and honey sandwiches, granola bars, soft drinks, some carrot sticks for her, an orange for me. Sometimes we would have the beach all to ourselves. Mom had this giant yellow towel that she used so often and kept for so long, the beach sand would sift through it. We'd lie down and feel the grains pressing warm and gritty against our backs. When the sun grew too hot, she'd jump up and sprint toward the water. Just before she hit it, her arms would flail in the air and she would shriek in anticipation of the cold and wet—then splash, she was gone. A moment later her head would break the surface, and she'd let her body ride in with the next wave. I'd grin and wait for her, feeling sand and sticky honey on my fingers and face. A moment later she'd sit next to me, dripping, her skin stark white and prickled with goose bumps.

When I'm ready, a few steps take me off the blacktop and onto the beach, where I tug off my shoes. The sand feels cool, and I like the way it squidges between my toes when I walk.

Things We Said Today

My destination lies just ahead: lifeguard stand number twelve. The Powers That Be do not allow beach guests to sit on the lifeguard stands. A sign appears on each one, right alongside the flimsy ladder you have to climb to get up top. The problem the Powers That Be face, of course, is that lifeguards won't be hired until June, seven months from now, and no one around here really cares one way or the other if I plant myself up there. The city does have a beach patrol, and the patrolmen do wear badges and guns, but I've learned they're more worried about drugs and alcohol than they are about some skinny kid sitting up on the lifeguard stand to watch the sun set. One of them sees me up there all the time, and he just waves to me as he goes zipping by on his dune buggy.

I huff my way to the base of the stand and start to climb the six rungs to the top. Once I'm there, the guitar case slips to the wood floor, Syke's leather jacket lands at my feet, and I suddenly feel like stretching. My arms reach out to the sun, and I'm standing on tiptoe. The muscles in my arms, shoulders, and legs tense up, then relax. After a moment I just let my legs fold at the knees so that I'm sitting.

I pop the latches and grab my guitar. The case has a little storage box on the inside for accessories, and I open this as well. My fingers dig into it and pull out my Pick Pocket, a flat leather pouch containing a half a dozen or so of my favorite tortoiseshell guitar picks. I don't worry about an amp. After all the time I've spent up here, I've gotten used to the twangy, wiry sound of an unamplified electric guitar. Good thing, too. My new attitude has saved me from a million arguments with Syke over which gets to be louder, my guitar or his television.

I start to play, but then I hesitate and look again across the ocean. I need another few minutes with the surf: the rush of the water, the cawing of the gulls, the sun like a warm wet towel against my face and arms, the air full of fish and salt and warm seaweed. I set the guitar down and draw my knees up, hugging them against my body.

A few moments later the guitar is in my lap again. A tingle of anger is always there inside me, though it had dimmed for a while as I looked out on the water. Now it comes back. The Telecaster gives me a bright, clean sound, but I imagine I'm plugged in, that the clean sound tears through my amp as a fuzzy scream of distortion. I love it, because I can hide behind that noise like it's a wall. I play a classic riff, one that pounds to the steady, machine-gun rhythm of punk. I'm not a big fan of punk, but it's angry music, and of course that's what I'm feeling. The only problem with playing unplugged is that I hear the music in my ears, but not in my bones. If I were playing through my little thirty-watt Pignose, or, even better, through the hundred-watt Marshall I keep in the garage to blow out the neighbors, the music would be slamming me in the chest right about now. Sometimes the music has to be that way, so loud it just pounds everything else out of you.

My eyes are closed, but I can still feel the sun, hear the surf, and taste the air. I slow down my playing a bit. My finger pulls up on the B string, bending the note into something cool and bluesy. I nod in time with the line I'm playing. I can hear a chord progression in my head, the foundation of a song I haven't yet written, and I'm vamping a solo over it. Thoughts of my mom slide away like the tide. As I play, I open my eyes and see that the bottom curve of that huge sun is just now touching the water. I watch it slip further, the Telecaster chiming in my ears, my fingers gently picking the sun down.

2

Two of Us

I can hear Syke's Softail when I'm still five houses away. Our garage door is open, and from inside comes the steady *potato-potato-potato* stutter of a Harley engine. It grows louder as I approach. At one point I hear it tear up to a roar as he gives the throttle a twist, but then it settles back down again. I find him on one knee, wrench sticking out from the back pocket of his jeans, his hands blackened to the wrists. The Softail is a big bike, but Syke is bigger. He used to ride a little Suzuki 750, until I told him he looked like he was sitting on one of those miniature ponies they let kids ride at the petting zoo. That's when he started saving up for the Harley. His back is to me, and in the garage the engine echoes like a thunderstorm, so he doesn't know I'm here. I reach past him, just far enough to let him see a girl's hand sticking out of the sleeve of his leather jacket, and snatch the near-empty bottle of beer standing next to him. I get it halfway to my mouth before he grabs it back. Syke stands six-foot-five, and he has the belly of a bear just before hibernation season, but he's impossibly quick.

"Hey, just kidding." I'm shouting over the noise, but I think it's the fact that I'm laughing that gets the idea across.

Syke's fingers are thick, and when he reaches up to shut off the engine, I can see shallow, bloody scratches on the knuckles. They seep, red and shiny, through the grease on his skin.

"Hey," he says.

"Hey."

Here comes the daily quiz. Where I've been. What I've been doing. I'm used to it, and though I can put on a real show of annoyance when he starts up, I actually kind of like it.

"How was school?"

I'm tired today, so I opt for tolerance. My answer is a shrug of my shoulders, but the jacket is so huge on me he doesn't catch it. "Awright," I tell him. "Vocab quiz in English. I passed—maybe a C."

He wipes his hands on a rag that's dirtier than they are. "Did you go to tutoring?"

"No."

He stops wiping, and I see the deep furrows between his eyes. He has a swipe of grease across the tip of his nose, and I have to work not to laugh when I see it. I lick my thumb and wipe it away, then kiss him on top of his bald head.

"How was your session with Dr. Artaud?" he asks.

"Awright."

Syke doesn't press me. He asks about the sessions because he thinks it's part of his job, but he sees the wall here. If I don't answer, he won't push.

Sometimes I come home and spill everything—every word, every feeling, every twirl of the pencil into Dr. Artaud's chin. Other times, like today, I don't much feel like talking about it. I think Syke has figured out my quiet days. He knows they mean I'm working through something. Today it's the song. I wish she hadn't brought it up. I know I need to write one for my mother, and the fact that I haven't—that I can't—presses down on me.

"Okay," I say, changing the subject, "now it's my turn." I point to the beer bottle. "What's with this?"

Two of Us

"My first and last of the week," says Syke. "And the Rams play the Steelers on Sunday. You gotta give me that, too."

After Mom died, I got pissy, shut myself up in my room, and tried to knock the walls down with my stereo system. Syke drank. He drank a lot. He wasn't a mean drunk; he'd just come home from work, make himself and me some dinner, then sit down in front of the television set until he emptied a six-pack—or maybe a bottle of something stronger. Then he'd either fall asleep in the chair or stagger off to bed, weepy-eyed. This went on about a month. I guess I was the first to come out of it, because after school one day I went to the cupboard where he kept all the liquor and one by one emptied the bottles into the sink. When he came home, he found I'd Scotch-taped and superglued the bottles together in the shape of a huge tower and left it in the middle of the living room. It looked like a fairy tale castle, only with labels. Syke turned almost purple, and I thought he might ground me for a month. Then he just sort of squeezed his eyes shut. He laughed, poked the tower with his finger to test its sturdiness, hugged me, then took me out to dinner and a movie.

Now we try to watch each other's back. He won't let me shut myself up too much or get too angry; I won't let him drink. He did negotiate one exception, though. On game days, he said, he gets a bottle of beer to go with his chili and Fritos—and though I don't exactly get how that combination works, I conceded the point: He gets a beer on the weekend. I figure working on his motorcycle in the garage probably fits into a similar macho-guy, sports-lover, motorcycle-riding, beer-drinking category, so I let this midweek lapse slide.

"Hey—trivia question," I say. "John Lennon wrote a song for his mother. What was it called?"

"'Julia'?"

"Nah, I'm thinking of another one. Post-Beatles. It's really bugging me."

He yanks the wrench from his back pocket and lets it land with a clatter in his toolbox. "You got me," he says. The latches on the toolbox close with a sharp, metallic snap, and Syke shoves it across the floor, underneath the workbench where he keeps it.

"C'mon," I say. "I'll make dinner."

He swigs the last of his beer and then stands, knees popping. "I'll help."

"You're not touching anything with those hands," I tell him.

He gives me a friendly swat to the back of my head. "Who said you could wear my jacket?"

It takes him about as long to clean up as it takes me to boil some noodles, heat up the jar of Ragu, and bake the prepackaged frozen meatballs. Later, when he comes in wearing a clean sweatshirt and jeans, his hands pink from scrubbing, he starts turning slices of toast into quickie garlic bread. I chop the lettuce and tomatoes for the salad; he handles the onion and bell peppers.

While we're eating, I see him twirl his fork absently in the spaghetti. Spaghetti is about all I can cook, which means we have it relatively frequently, and I know very well how Syke eats it: big, swirled gobs of noodles on the end of his fork, half-eaten bread at his plate soaked with sauce, red-spattered napkin in his lap. Right now he's just latching onto a few strands of noodles with his fork and playing with them.

"What's wrong?" I ask.

"Oh, nothing—nothing," he says. "I've just been thinking."

A speck of Parmesan cheese clings to the hairs of his goatee. I point to it. "You got a thing…"

He dabs it with his napkin. "Thanks. Working on the bike, I was thinking...and well, we'd been talking about the garage and the boxes and all..."

He stops there, his voice trailing off like mine does when I can't come up with the right lie. I can sense what's coming. Syke married my mom only seven years ago. He'd never been married before, he'd never had any kids, and for the most part he just kind of fumbles through being a dad. For him, being a parent is a little like being the new kid on the block and stepping into his first-ever pickup baseball game. Still, Syke sees the pitches coming and takes his best swing, and I love him for it.

"It's okay," I tell him. "It's not too soon."

I know I'm right when I say this, because my stomach doesn't feel queasy and my heart is right in my chest where it belongs.

The boxes in the garage belonged to my mother. She could never throw anything away, and when she and Syke bought this place, all the junk she'd saved went into U-Haul boxes, which are now stacked three high against the garage wall. Syke's been talking about going through them—cleaning up, cleaning out, selling, throwing away. I went nuts the first time he mentioned it and threw my old softball mitt at him, but that was weeks ago.

Right now I think about my knees, about the way they felt during my therapy session. They're solid now. "It's okay, Syke. Really. You're busy with work. I can do it."

"Tomorrow?" he asks.

"Tomorrow. Right after school."

He jabs a meatball with his fork and points at my chin with it. "You got a thing."

Pepperland

I slog through my homework assignments—a rough draft of a 500-word persuasive essay (mine runs 328, with tiny little numbers in the margins where I've counted), ten problems in geometry, and a chapter's worth of reading in Western Civilizations. I skip the reading, figuring my friend Dooley will do it and fill me in.

The music on my stereo makes me dreamy. I tell Syke I can work with it on, that it doesn't distract me, but of course it does. I can shut it out long enough to write a sentence or two, but then a guitar lick catches my ear, and I have to stop and listen. Sometimes I try to imagine my hands on the neck of my Tele, feeling around for the lick like a prospector panning for gold. I have to do this sort of practice in my head. If I actually pick up the guitar, it's all over. No homework gets done, and Star shows up at school with an empty notebook and an idiot grin.

I scrub out a math problem with my eraser and toss my pencil down. Something's been niggling at my brain. It's the Lennon song again. I can't let go of it. It should leap out at me, like my cousin's name or my locker number at school, but it doesn't. I know I've heard it…something mellow sounding. Or maybe it's harder, more rocky. I can't stand not knowing. I throw open my bedroom door and rush to the living room, where Syke is eating ice cream and watching *M*A*S*H*. His big Kenwood receiver sits in the corner, wires connected to speakers the size of little refrigerators. Scattered on a shelf above the system are some six dozen cassette tapes. I start rampaging through them, tracking my finger along the edges and angrily yanking the ones that are filed upside down or unreadable. *Yellow Submarine*, with its bright colors and images of Pepperland, catches my eye, but it's not what I want.

"Syke," I say, "you got any Lennon?"

"Dunno," he says. "Probably—hey, what are you doing?"

I go through them once, twice, but can't find what I'm

looking for. Without answering Syke, I start jamming the loose tapes back into their spots, and I think I crack one of the cases.

"You'd have a better shot going through..."

He stops there. He was going to say "through your mother's collection," but he cut himself off. He *always* cuts himself off. "Mom" and "mother" are black-magic words, not to be uttered. Anyway, I'm already gone. Syke's voice turns into background noise, like tape hiss. A drawer in my bedroom has about a jillion cassettes in it—some mine, some my mother's. I yank it right out and set it on the floor in front of me. My hands are moving like a fast-food cook's—darting here and there, pulling out a tape and tossing it back down—but there's no obvious order to what I'm doing. The fourth tape I hold up isn't right, and I slam it down on the floor. A *gah!* sound bursts from my throat.

I feel it now. It starts as a little burning in the center of my chest, then it spreads until I can feel the heat in my face and neck and down to the tips of my fingers. After two months of therapy, I know the explosion is coming before it happens. A little part of me can even stand back and watch, take mental notes on the crazy girl.

The burning is all over me. I grab the drawer and turn it upside down, causing a huge clatter of falling plastic. I shove the drawer aside. Now the tapes are a glittery pile in front of me. I grab them one at a time and hold them up to the light— *not it...not it...not it*—then toss them aside. The first few I toss gently, but then I throw hard, not caring, spinning them like Frisbees. *Shoosh!* A tape skids across carpet. *Tack!* One hits the door, and the case breaks. I'm using both hands, so the sounds overlap one another. *Not it...not it...* I'm running out of tapes, but my hands are shaking and my skin—face, neck, chest, arms, fingers—tingles and burns. I'm there now, in that place where I can see what I'm doing, but it's as if someone else is doing it. I yank out another drawer and swing it like a base-ball bat, sending my underwear, socks, and bras flying across the room. I'm on my feet now, pulling at my bedding until it comes off. I hurl it against the wall. "Gah!" I spin around. My hands find something, my bedside table, and shove hard. It topples, the corner cutting a wedge in the drywall, the lamp cracking against the floor and blinking out. I scatter papers off my desk, knock books off my shelf. My hands find the curtains and tear them from the window. *Enough. Enough.* I can't breathe. I whirl. I stumble on my own mess, and my shoulder hits the wall. The jolt hurts my neck. *Enough.* I roll so my back is against the wall, my shoulder blades pressing hard into it, and then I let myself slide down to the floor. I'm shaking, and for the first time I can feel that my face is wet; tears are absolutely pouring down my cheeks and my nose. My upper lip is sticky. I draw my knees up. I slide my sleeve across my face. The burning fades to a warmth.

I breathe.

Syke is standing in the doorway.

He stares at me, at the broken tapes, at the dings in the walls, at the pile of clothes and bedding, at the curtain rod hanging from the window frame like a broken tree limb. He sees it all and understands none of it. His hand covers his mouth as though to hold back all the wrong words that might spill out.

I'm sobbing. My whole body shakes. The room feels freez-ing cold.

Syke moves slowly across the mess, careful not to step on anything breakable, and scoots down to the floor next to me. I hear him grunt with the effort, the big bear. His arm goes around me, and my head drops to his shoulder. He just sits there hugging me, because he doesn't know what else to do.

3

And Your Bird Can Sing

On the way to school, a paper wad lands in my hair. I crumple it and toss it back over my shoulder, somewhere in the general direction of the person who threw it. It's your basic mayhem-and-carnage bus ride. Kids yell, laugh, sing; the racket mixes with the rumble of the bus engine until my head aches.

I stare out the window, past the girl who sits next to me. She looks twelve or thirteen. She has brown hair cut to chin length and pulled back with two plastic barrettes shaped like butterflies. I watch as she pulls a weird little box from her purse. Silver letters on the side of the box spell the word "Sony." She touches something and a door on the box pops open. Her hand dips into her purse again and comes out with a cassette tape, which she slips inside the box before closing the door. Now I'm fascinated. It's clearly a cassette player of some kind, but I don't see any speakers. How does she—?

Oh.

She plugs a wire into the side of the box. A little headset, nothing but plastic and pink foam pads, snaps over her ears. When she presses Play, I hear a metallic hiss and the ticking rhythm of a drumbeat.

"What is that?" I ask.

Pepperland

She presses the Stop button and tugs one of the earpieces away. "Hmm?"

"Your tape player—or whatever. What is it?"

"It's a Sony Soundabout," she says. "Haven't you heard one yet?"

I shake my head.

She pulls the headset off and places it over my ears. The pads tickle, then settle in. She smiles a smile that says *watch this*. Then she presses...

Oh my God.

Billy Joel is singing in my head. The song is "My Life," and the guitar is in my left ear, the bass thumps in my right, and Billy Joel is *singing in my freaking head*. This is not just stereo. It's *real*. He's five feet away, almost chewing on the microphone, eyes closed. *I don't need you to worry for me, 'cuz I'm all right...* I'm in a recording studio, and he's on the other side of the glass, waving at me. Backup singers chime in on the bridge. They're right in front of me. All this in a box no bigger than my old AM/FM transistor radio.

The girl with the butterfly barrettes laughs at the expression on my face. She carefully draws the headset from my ears and places it back on her own. "Cool, huh?" she asks.

"Yes," I say, though she can't hear me. "Cool." But I'm wrong. The little box plugged into her head is not cool. It's the Apollo moon landing. It's the discovery of penicillin. It's a new world.

And I can't wait to tell Dooley.

The bus squeals when it stops in front of the school, the air brakes hissing like a tire going flat. I'm standing at the doors before they open.

I can see Dooley. He sits on the edge of a brick planter that circles an oak tree donated by the graduating class of 1954. He meets me here every morning, even in the rain. He never seems to have a schoolbook with him, only his oversized art pad full of pencil sketches. Dooley is the best artist I've ever known. He's also into origami. Right now his attention is on a sheet of paper and on the careful folds he's making in it. He hasn't heard the bus pull up, or he *has* heard but is too intent on the paper to care. His arms and legs are long; the joints seem to break sharply instead of bend. When he sits this way, all hunched over, his elbows and knees are big knobs on the ends of sticks. His hair is neck-length and the color of straw. It looks like a tiny haystack as he leans over—folding, folding.

"Hey," I say.

"Hey there." He doesn't look at me. The paper in front of him is a stiff sheet of blank art paper—good, Dooley says, for holding a tight crease. He's folded it down the middle and now takes a corner of it, bending it down once, then again, and drawing his fingernail against these new folds to sharpen them. Then he begins working on another corner.

"What's it going to be?" I ask.

"A masterpiece of engineering," he says. "You'll see." He still hasn't looked at me.

I watch Dooley turn down a corner, measuring with his eyes. Then comes more folding. Two shapes, vaguely winglike, stick out on either side now. Folding…folding…another pause to measure his progress. Soon a neck dips below the body and curves back up. A head appears, sharp and triangular.

"It looks like a pterodactyl," I tell him.

"Umm-hmmm," he says. "And more."

I watch for another five minutes, my epiphany with the Sony Soundabout temporarily forgotten. Dooley makes another fold along the body of his bird, stiffening it and adding weight below the wings. "Now pay attention," he says. He slips the bird into his shirt pocket.

Dooley is tall and skinny and slumps, but he surprises me with his quickness. He leaps to his feet, his arm catching the lowest branch of the oak. He swings himself around it and up, knees circling another branch and sending him even higher. He scampers—I've never seen him scamper—to the highest branch he trusts to hold his weight, maybe a dozen feet in the air. And before I can shout his name or tell him how stupid he is, he draws his arm back and lets the bird fly.

"Dooley—!"

I can't finish. I'm watching. The pterodactyl soars from the tree and glides to an altitude of twenty feet or so. It dips, catches a current, and keeps going. It banks and heads toward the quad, where several students look up, following it with their eyes. It catches another current of air and sails higher, the weight in the nose keeping it balanced and straight. Another dip. The bird wavers, slows, and drops in altitude. Ten feet, seven, five…. It's just a white speck now. I can barely see it as it glides to the grass and settles some thirty yards from Dooley and me and the oak tree.

"Yes!" Dooley whoops, pumps his fist several times, then swings down from the branch. "Did you see that?" he shouts. "Did you see? I've been working on the design forever, but I didn't want to show it off until it was ready."

"You've created the perfect paper airplane?"

He whoops again. It's the only answer I get from him.

He can't contain himself. He has to run across the grass to retrieve his bird. I walk behind him quietly, letting him put space between us in case he does something really embarrassing. Another boy races him to the white speck in the grass, but Dooley gets there first. He snatches it up, dabs it with his T-shirt to remove some drops of dew, smoothes out a wing, and carries it back to me in cupped hands. It looks like a dead dove.

"Was that amazing or what?" he asks. He's grinning at me, his whole face lit up with his accomplishment. I figure a dad in a maternity ward waiting room probably grins like this. Dooley has just fathered a child.

"Yes," I say, "it's amazing."

I want to tell him about the girl on the bus, about the magic of real stereo music playing from that tiny box directly into my ears, but I don't. The bell rings, so we just walk together in silence. Each morning deserves only one dose of amazing, I guess, and today's belongs to Dooley.

After school we meet at my house. Dooley plays bass, but he and his mom live in an apartment. I've got a garage and a Marshall stack and neighbors who don't get home until six o'clock. End of discussion.

I'm in the garage, setting up mikes and plugging the Marshall into a wall outlet when he pulls up in his car—a '74 AMC Gremlin. He hauls his bass out of the backseat and walks toward me, the guitar balanced on his left shoulder. He doesn't have a case for it, and it has a half-inch chip in the lower bout where he dropped it once. He's layered stickers across the face of it: Peter Frampton, The Clash, Bad Company, the Sierra Club, and a simple black one with white lettering that says "I'm schizophrenic, and so am I."

"Here—I made this," he says. He hands me one of his origami creations. At first I think it's a horse, but then I see the spike coming from its forehead.

"A unicorn! Thank you." I let it stand in my palm for a moment, admiring it, then set it on top of my amp. Later it'll join the rest of the zoo. "Come on," I tell him. "Grab the bass amp and plug in."

We kill an hour. Dooley plays decent bass, and I can hammer out some lead licks, but we both know we desperately need a drummer to keep us together. Our tastes don't quite mesh either. I try not to laugh when he gets to the "buh-buh-buh-baby" part in "You Ain't Seen Nothin' Yet." And he tolerates my shouting out something by Heart or Pat Benatar. Really, Dooley is pretty generous. We've both figured out that our jam sessions are considerably more for my benefit than for his. I can lose myself here. I close my eyes when I sing, and except for the steady thump of his bass, I hardly know he's with me. That sounds awful, but it's true.

I'm in the middle of "Hit Me with Your Best Shot" when I remember my conversation with Syke. I stop playing, and Dooley grinds to a halt a bar or two behind me.

"What's wrong?"

I slip my guitar over my head and tug off the strap. "Aw, I forgot I told Syke I'd go through some of these boxes today. Clear some old stuff out."

"Your mom's stuff?"

I'm snapping down the latches of my guitar case when Dooley says this. The last latch sounds like a shot going off in my head. "Um...yeah."

"I'll help."

"No, really," I say. "You don't have to. Besides, you might miss your dinner."

He leans his guitar against the wall, steadying it to make sure it doesn't tip over. "Even better," he says. "Gives me an excuse to stop at McDonald's and skip Mom's macaroni and cheese."

The boxes are stacked against the far wall. They've been there forever—well, since Syke and my mom got married when I was nine. Now they're sagging under their own weight. I can't imagine anything inside them is important—

after all, Mom never seemed to miss anything from them—so this should be easy. All I have to do is take a few steps forward and grab one, any one, and sift through it. Toss. Keep. Toss. Keep. But I'm stuck where I stand.

Dooley moves past me in a hurry. He's tall, and his arms are long white skinny sticks. He grabs a box from the top of the nearest stack and drops it on the floor at my feet. Now I guess I have to do something. I sit down next to it, slowly drawing my knees up and wrapping my arms around myself. I can feel my body rocking slightly, my weight tipping forward a few inches then falling back.

On the side of the box, in my mother's handwriting, is the word "junk." I can't take my eyes off it. Mom's *J* has a cross-bar that swirls up from left to right, with a little flaring hook at the end. The rest of the letter dips down like a saxophone, and it's three times the size of the *u*, *n*, and *k*. Dooley plunks himself down next to me and reaches for the box's flaps, which are crossed over themselves to keep the box shut. His hand locks onto one flap and starts to tug, but then he stops and looks at me. It's occurred to him I might have something to say about his leaping into my mom's stuff.

"Oops. Is this okay?" he asks. "Or do you want to go first?"

I wave my hand. *Go. It's nothing.*

He waits another second or two, watching me just to make sure I don't change my mind, then yanks on the flap. The box makes a shredding sound then pops open.

Peering past Dooley's shoulder, I watch as he pulls out a few of the items inside: old letters, a faded ticket stub to a Gordon Lightfoot concert, an old-style reel of audiotape, a four-inch-long button in the shape of a guitar (with Paul McCartney's face plastered over it), Mom's old glasses with the black Buddy Holly frames, and a thick book with a brown, imitation leather cover.

"Let me see that," I say, pointing.

Dooley hands it over. On the front where the title would be is the word *Kaleidoscope* spelled out in gold letters that have begun to chip and flake. In the lower corner, also in gold, are the words *Franklin Roosevelt Senior High School, 1964*.

"A yearbook?" Dooley asks.

"The year my mom graduated," I tell him.

"She had you when she was in high school?"

"The summer after," I tell him. "And shut up."

The book crackles when I open it, and I can see little flecks of gold on my fingers. I riffle the pages. Moisture has gotten to them over the years, and a few stick together. A little tug separates them.

"Oh...my...*gawsh*."

The girls have neck-length hairstyles that sweep back and out like antique Barbie dolls'. Most of them wear plaid skirts with long pleats or dresses with dainty Peter Pan collars. The guys wear cardigan sweaters, loafers, and short-sleeved shirts buttoned to the neck. In a photo of a high school dance, a boy and girl stand three feet apart, hands touching. Her skirt swirls around her, like she's just spun away from him. She's all motion and trust. I can tell just by looking that she knew his hand would be there to take hers, that his fingers would lock onto hers and draw her back to him, and I'm a little jealous.

"Hey, look," says Dooley. "I'm Elvis Costello."

He's wearing the big glasses with the black plastic frames. I laugh, snatch them from his face, and hide them behind my back. Now it's a wrestling match. His hands are like snakes, darting around me first one way and then the other, trying to grab the glasses again. One of his elbows accidentally jabs me in the shoulder. "Hey—hey, come on," I say. "Knock it off." He reaches behind me again, and I shove him away with the flat of my palm. "Dooley! I said knock it off, okay? I'm looking at this."

I'm not really mad, but my tone gets him. He hunkers down next to me and gazes silently at the book.

While we were messing around, several of the pages flipped over. The one staring up at me now has writing on it—blue and black ink, little paragraphs floating below pictures. The students on these pages wear dark gowns and mortarboards. The smiles are huge and gleaming, with a hint of graduation panic.

To Cat—Remember the bonfire party on the beach? Cruising in my dad's T-bird with the top down and the radio up? The fly in your chili cheese fries? I'm still laughing.
                                    Best friends 4-ever, Maureen.

Cat, what's the answer to number twelve? Just kidding. Could not have made it through algebra II without you.
                                    Yours truly and sincerely, Douglas.

Dear Cat—hey, you absolutely have to call me when you get to Palo Alto! I don't know whether to hug you good-bye or just be mad at you for going off to Stanford without me. It's all so scary, isn't it? Promise you'll write.
                                    Love, Helen.

I find dozens like these. My hands grip the book more tightly as I read them. I knew my mom well, but these little notes contain secrets she never told me. She was voted "Best Personality." She played the part of Emily in a senior class production of *Our Town*. She smoked a cigarette, and it made her throw up. She got detention when a janitor caught her kissing a boy in a maintenance closet.

"Like a painting of your mom," says Dooley.

"Huh?"

He riffles the pages, revealing more photos, more good-bye

notes. "You know, like small brush strokes, but all together they make a picture."

I nod. "Yeah."

My hand turns the pages slowly. The photos appear in alphabetical order, and I know what's coming. She's in the middle of the page—second from the left, three rows down. Mom's smile is the one I remember—warm, crooked, sincere, eyebrows slightly raised like she knows something you don't. The tilt of her chin makes her look less afraid, less overwhelmed than the others. Here's something I don't like: Her eyes are smaller and not quite as bright as I expected. I'm a little mad that the picture doesn't live up to my memory of her. Maybe it's the dorky glasses. She's wearing them in her senior photo, and I love her for that. They're like a big structure built over her nose and around her eyes—like a bridge no one bothered to finish. I feel my mouth tugging up in a smile. At the same time I feel this warm prickling in the corners of my eyes, and I know I have to put the book down. I'll read it later—all of it.

"Let's look at something else," I say.

I toss the book to Dooley, and he fumbles it. The covers flap open; the pages rustle. Something slips from inside and lands on the floor. It's an envelope. I pluck it from the concrete with my thumb and forefinger. It's the most God-awful-looking thing—white turned dirty yellow and dotted with a psychedelic paisley pattern. In the upper corner of the envelope is some familiar handwriting. Blue ink. Swirling letters. My mother's name. Beneath it is her address—the old one in Vermont, where she grew up. A five-cent postage stamp sits an inch or so from the envelope's edge, as though my mom had intended to add more postage later.

"What is it?" Dooley asks.

"Looks like a letter."

In the center of the envelope is a single name with no address. I see the same *J* my mother wrote on the outside of the cardboard box and the letters that follow, but I can't bring myself to say the name aloud. My fingernail traces it instead. The prickling in my eyes turns to pure heat, and I can feel them tearing up.

Dooley, of course, senses none of this. He just spits out the name like it's something he's found in a phone book. "Hey," he says, "John Lennon."

I laugh, then sniffle. "Yeah."

"So it's what—a fan letter or something?"

"Probably," I say. "I guess she wrote it, then realized she didn't know where to mail it."

"You gonna open it?"

I turn the envelope over and work my thumbnail underneath the sealed flap. I'm about to tear it open, but then something stops me. Maybe, I think, my mom's dumb teenager fantasies were her own business. If she had a crush on a Beatle, so what? And if she keeled over in a faint at a concert, or shut down her whole life for fifteen minutes while she watched *The Ed Sullivan Show,* or pressed a lipstick kiss onto a fan letter— well, Dooley doesn't have to know about it. I know my mom. Her favorite album was *Help!* Her favorite song was "In My Life." Her favorite Beatle was John. I smooth out the bump I've made in the flap and slip the letter back under the cover of the book.

"Maybe later," I say.

That evening, after Syke and I have eaten, I hole up in my room. He worries when I pull my hermit routine, especially when he doesn't hear any music playing, but I just feel like being alone and quiet tonight. Mom's yearbook sits on my shelf. Her old glasses rest on my dressing table. The letter, balanced upright, leans against my makeup mirror. Sprawled on my bed, I stare at it. Seeing her handwriting, her name, makes me hear her voice in my head.

I close my eyes and see her....

Mom doesn't look well. The doctors allowed her to come home from the hospital, but the fact that she's here terrifies me. I want to believe she's getting better. Isn't that why people come home from a hospital, because they're better? But I already know—and I don't *want* to know—that she's home for another reason.

I'm standing in the doorway of her bedroom, watching as Syke feeds her. His weight on the edge of the bed makes the mattress tip down like the edge of a leaky boat. He balances a tray on one knee while his free hand dips a spoon into a bowl of soup. I watch the spoon shake as it makes the trip to my mother's mouth, spilling a few drops on the quilt. "Sorry," Syke says, "sorry." He lays a napkin across her chest, then cups one hand under her chin and tips the spoon against her lips. Mom makes a muffled sound, like the soup's too hot or it's coming too fast. A line of broth trails down her chin, and Syke dabs it away with a napkin.

I just watch. My mother's skin is white with hints of blue around the eyes and temples. Her pretty hair is gone, so now she covers her head with a scarf. I've seen her twirl a corner of the scarf around her finger when she doesn't see me watching, just the way I twirl my hair when I'm talking to a guy. She moans. The room reeks of a stomach-churning mix of cherry cough syrup and rubbing alcohol and chicken soup, and it all hits me at once. My hands grip the doorframe, and I lean into it. Watching her now, I want to reach inside my mother and tear out every bad cell with my hands. I want to brush her forehead with my fingers, a magic healing touch, and watch her hair grow back and the color return to her cheeks. I want to wave a wand and see thirty pounds fill out her body. And since I can't make these miracles happen, I'm left with a horrible urge: I want to run. I want to slam the door to my room and crank up my stereo until the sound is so loud it crushes everything I'm feeling.

More than anything, this last desire makes me hate myself.

"Hey, baby," she says.

"Hi, Mom." I walk over to the bed and take the tray. "I can do this," I tell Syke. He leaves for the kitchen, and I start spoon-feeding my mother. Her eyes stare into mine, trying to figure out what I'm thinking and feeling. The answer is I don't know. The momentary desire to run is gone, but what's left is just too big. I can't get my mind around it.

"Reminds me of when you were a baby," she says. "I fed you in your high chair. It had a teddy bear on it."

"Winnie the Pooh," I tell her. I dip the spoon in the soup again. "Was I a good baby?"

"You threw your Cheerios onto the floor."

This makes me laugh. "A brat even then."

"No," she says. "I think you liked the sound the bowl made when it hit the linoleum."

Dip the spoon. Bring it to her mouth. Tip slowly. Catch the spill.

"How was school?" she asks.

Pepperland

Not much to say. I can't remember what happened in a single class, so I think about the morning break, passing periods, lunch, the parts of the day when neat little nothings happen. A guy's face pops into my mind: Sean O'Doul—I call him Dooley—bought me a Coke and sat with me. Yesterday he slipped me a note. *I'm bored,* it said. *You?*

"I think this guy likes me," I tell her.

"Is he nice?" she asks. It's the same question every time I talk about guys. This time her hand flops against my knee as she asks, and her eyes stay with mine. Something inside them is all lit up.

"I dunno," I confess. "He's kind of a dork."

Dip the spoon. Bring it to her mouth…

"Don't write off every dork," she says. Her voice is dry leaves blowing across concrete. "They're the ones who end up rich." Here she laughs a little too hard, coughs, then laughs again.

My smart mouth can't be contained. "Wasn't *that* funny," I say.

"No. Not that." She takes several deep breaths. "Some soup came up my nose!"

Bedsprings creak as she rolls back and forth, laughing again, and I can't help myself. I lose it too. Soup spills over the edge of the bowl and onto the sheet, and I have to set the tray down before it's all in our laps, a sloppy puddle of noodles and chicken bits and celery slices. Our laughter sounds like bells.

The next twenty minutes pass this way. Stupid questions. Stupid answers. More laughter. If she weren't dying, it would be perfect.

4

A Day in the Life

The letter is still staring at me when I wake up the next morning. The letters of my mother's name are like the eyes in a painting, following me around the room as I rush to get dressed. Jeans. Wrinkled sweatshirt. My toe pokes through a hole in my sock. I'm in a hurry, and I don't much care how I look today. My hair, still damp from the shower, clings to my head and neck, so I grab a brush and blow-dryer. I can't seem to focus on the mirror, though. The envelope. The name. I finally toss everything aside and yank my hair into a ponytail. I shove a pen and a pack of Juicy Fruit in my pocket. I grab my backpack. As I head out, I brush the envelope with my hand. *Bye, Mom, I'll catchya later.*

"I'm gone, Syke."

He grunts to let me know he's heard me. From behind the bathroom door his electric shaver spits and hums.

The bus arrives just as I run up to the corner. As I step on, I look around for the little girl with Billy-Joel-in-a-Box. I push aside a little flare of disappointment when I don't see her. The bus lurches, and I have to grab onto a steel pole to steady myself. Then I spy an empty seat. Treasure. When I find an empty one, I always sit on the aisle side and place my back-pack next to me. Often, if I put out the right vibe, no one will even ask me to scoot over. Here's the trick: You have to be completely quiet, look a little sullen, and make no eye contact with anyone who's just getting on. It's great. The more I want to be left alone, the better it seems to work. The seat stays mine, and mine alone, until the bus hits the school parking lot.

Dooley is not waiting for me at the oak tree.

I look for him. He's not in the quad, he's not in the cafeteria loading up on chocolate chip cookies, he's not in the library. I finally find him at his locker. He stands there with the door open, pressing his forehead against the top of the locker opening, like he's just finished banging his head there a couple of times. His eyes are closed. I wait a few seconds before speaking, but he doesn't move.

"Hey...Dooley?"

He turns to the sound of my voice and opens his eyes. They're ringed with red. His skin is flushed and his cheeks seem a little hollow. "What's the matter?" I ask. I can see inside the open locker, and everything looks normal—for him. A copy of my sophomore class picture is taped to the inside of the door. His books are stacked neatly. His colored pencils and pastel crayons, in their little vinyl packages, lie on top of the stack. His best drawings—a male gymnast swinging over parallel bars, a superhero in tights and black cape, a craggy-faced soldier—line the inside walls.

"Dooley...?" I ask.

He says nothing, just slams the locker door closed with enough force to make the whole bank of lockers hum. There, painted down the outside of the door, is a single word: FAGGOT. Dooley makes a low sound in his throat and presses his forearm against the letters. He rubs at them with his shirtsleeve, harder and harder, until the door squeaks and rattles. Dooley's not even smudging the paint. I place my hand on his elbow to stop him.

A Day in the Life

"C'mon," I say. "We'll find the custodian. She'll have something that'll take it off."

He slams his fist against the door. "I know who did this," he says under his breath. "I know who it was."

"Okay," I say.

"I *know* it. He's been poking around at this for a couple of weeks now. You know, kind of saying it without really saying it?"

Dooley strides down the hall with his head down and his shoulders hunched, looking a little like a scarecrow. I can feel him holding back so I can keep up with him. We turn a corner, heading toward the office, and run into a hall so crowded that we have to thread our way down the center of it. Dooley is mumbling under his breath. Strings of phrases start and stop, but all I hear with any clarity is the punch of breath that precedes each one. From behind, his neck looks flushed and angry, but hardly anyone turns and stares at us as we pass.

Then Dooley stops, and I walk right smack into him. My nose lands between his shoulder blades. "Ow! Whadja...?"

He's staring at some guy who stands at a locker about ten feet away. The guy is shorter than Dooley, fatter around the middle, and has brown hair that falls to his jawline. The hair is dirty, and the kid's face is pocked from old acne scars. His eyes bother me—they're set just a little too closely together. He's standing in front of some girl who's saying "I gotta go!" I struggle for a moment, but the guy's name finally comes— Farris...Farris Tidwell. He slams his locker shut and turns in time to catch Dooley staring at him. He grins viciously, kind of like the way a dog appears to be grinning when it opens its mouth to show some teeth. He spreads his arms wide—*What? Why are you looking at me?*—and does this really lame limp-wristed gesture with his hand.

Then he mouths the word painted on Dooley's locker.

Dooley shoves one guy out of his way and takes three steps toward the fat kid. I see his arm go up and his huge, bony hand—like a caveman's weapon, a rock lashed to the end of a club. It arcs toward the kid's face. But Dooley is tall and clumsy and moving too fast. He's off balance. Farris sees the punch coming and steps to the side, letting the fist brush by his face. He gives a hard shove to Dooley's shoulder—in the direction Dooley is already moving—and it's all over. Dooley smashes face-first into the lockers. His head bounces off one of the locker doors, denting it, and his knees sort of break underneath him. He just collapses to the linoleum. Blood runs from his nose, and I see three red lines, from the locker vents, cutting across his left cheek.

"Fight!" someone shouts, and in a second a crowd of a dozen students surrounds us. They're all shouting, not for one fighter or the other, but for the fight itself: entertainment.

Farris stands over Dooley, still smiling. "D'ja see that?" he shouts. "D'ja see this guy come up and try to hit me for no reason?" Dooley still lies on the floor, hands cupping his nose. "He threw the first punch, right? You all saw that?" A few kids in the crowd shout their agreement. Farris Tidwell takes this as permission to continue the fight. While Dooley rolls on the floor in front of him, Farris draws his boot back and delivers a solid kick to Dooley's stomach. I see my friend's body lift a little when the kick lands, then settle back to the floor. Dooley turns over and makes horrible hiccupping sounds, trying to catch his breath. His eyes bulge.

Someone whistles his appreciation. Farris is nodding, smiling, holding up his arms like a comic enjoying his own joke. He's having such a good time, I figure he'll kick Dooley again, so I step forward. I'm not really thinking. I'm just looking at Dooley and feeling the tingling in my chest.

A Day in the Life

"Hey, Farris?"

He turns at the sound of my voice. I'm already moving. My backpack has been hanging from my arm, heavy with my English and social studies books, and I swing it just as Farris Tidwell's eyes land on me. I hit him flush in the face, smacking his head back. When his shoulders hit the bank of lockers, I hear a sound like metal trash cans falling over. Behind me, the laughter and giggles turn to shrieks. I hear footsteps thudding against the linoleum, locker doors slamming, voices hissing. Everyone runs.

"Enough! Break it up!" Mrs. Ortiz, whose classroom is just up the hall, steps in front of me and places her hands on my shoulders. "Move back, young lady," she says, "and wait right over there." She turns, fists notched at her hips, and waits for the two boys to haul themselves to their feet. Dooley's breath is still hitching a little in his throat, and the red lines are a little brighter across his cheekbones. He presses one hand against his ribs and stands next to me. Farris slips getting to his feet and bangs his knee against the linoleum. Half his face is pink.

"And Mr. Tidwell," says the teacher. "Wonders never cease."

Mrs. Ortiz is a big woman whose laugh—when she *is* laughing, and right now she's not—you can hear halfway down the hall. She wears a cherry-red sweater with little books and apples and pencils embroidered on it. Even so, she manages to scare the crap out of me. She points her finger down the corridor like the Ghost of Christmas Yet to Come.

"March," she says.

I squeeze my eyes shut for a second and swallow the groan in my throat. I know where we're headed, but I also know the issue won't end there. It won't end with the vice principal's discipline report. It won't even end when they call Syke to come get me.

Oh, I know where it will end.

☆

"What do *you* think happened?"

Dr. Artaud swivels back and forth in her chair as she asks the question. Her notebook rests on one knee, and she riffles the page edges with her thumb so they sound like a fly buzzing.

Instead of responding, I pick at a thread that sticks out of the seam of the leather couch next to me. I sniffle and run my finger underneath my nose, though I don't have allergies and my nose is not runny. Then, since these activities don't use up much time, I let my eyes take a tour of her office: the empty blotter on her desk; the framed poster from a Parisian dance review on the wall, full of blotchy reds, oranges, and yellows; the psychology texts with scary titles like *Diagnostic and Statistical Manual on Mental Disorders, 23rd Edition.* My gaze finally lands on the diplomas hanging just inside the door. Her undergraduate degree. Her postgraduate degree. Her doctorate. Her license to practice from the Board of Psychology. They remind me of a word puzzle I learned in the seventh grade.

"Hey, what's this?" I ask. I grab one of those weird sticky notes from Dr. Artaud's desk and scribble a little design on it. Then I slap it down in front of her, running my finger along the adhesive to stick the note to her desktop. The design looks like this...

$$\frac{0}{\begin{array}{c} \text{BA} \\ \text{MA} \\ \text{PhD} \end{array}}$$

A Day in the Life

"Three degrees below zero," says Dr. Artaud. She peels the note up and slowly crumples it in her fist. Her hands are tiny, her knuckles like little sharp rocks under the skin. "You haven't answered my question, Star."

"Nothing," I tell her. "Really, nothing. I just get mad sometimes."

She scribbles something onto her notepad. "I see. This morning you bashed a student in the face with your backpack. The other night you threw clothes across the room, tore bedding, knocked a hole in the wall, broke—by your father's account—about two dozen cassette tapes. 'Mad' is a bit of an understatement, wouldn't you say?"

I don't say. My thumb and forefinger play with the loose thread some more. Today is not my regular session. After what happened this morning, Syke made a call and arranged for an extra appointment. He's sitting in the waiting room right now. Syke and Dr. Artaud wouldn't let me bring my guitar into the session, so I have nothing to hide behind except hair and attitude, and those just aren't enough. I have to concentrate so that I don't sound whiny. "I told you about Farris. I had to do *something*. And as for the other night...it was *nothing*. I just lost my temper."

"Have you ever lost your temper like that before?"

"No."

I'm lying. About three weeks ago I came home from school tired and cranky. My head hurt. I was hungry, and for some reason my stomach was set on Sloppy Joes. I tore the shrink-wrap off the hamburger, but when I went to the cupboard, I realized we were out of mix. That's when I lost it. I started to feel the way I felt the other night—the tingling in my chest, the heat all over my skin, and the freaky feeling that I was watching a crazy person and the crazy person was me. I hurled the

39

hamburger into the trash can, threw a chair down, and pounded my fist and forearm against the refrigerator door. Syke never would have known, except I bruised myself.

"And how is your arm feeling?" Dr. Artaud asks.

My face flushes. It didn't even occur to me that he might have told the shrink about the fridge incident. "I'm sorry," I tell her. "I didn't mean to lie."

"Actually, I think you did mean to," says the doctor. "But I understand you're still a little reticent about sharing." She's not angry. She's just stating the point, which makes it all the harder to get angry in return. She lays the notebook aside. "I'm just curious as to the reason, Star. Did you think these outbursts weren't important? Or did you know they were important and decide you didn't want to deal with them? You can take your time answering, but I'm betting on door number two."

I shrug.

Dr. Artaud nods, accepting my response. "Okay then, answer me this, Star. Why are you here?"

I scratch my nose. Run my fingers through my hair. Rock back and forth on the floor. "Because Syke made me come," I tell her. "That's all."

"And you don't think you need to be here—or that you need some help?"

For several seconds I say nothing. Before my mom died I'd been angry, but I'd never exploded—certainly not over cassette tapes or Sloppy Joes.

I'm tired of this. I'm tired of leather couches and Dr. Artaud's practiced, soothing voice; I'm tired of her diplomas and the scritch of her pen. But maybe she's right. Maybe I do need her.

Finally I hear myself whispering, "I'm like...disconnected."

She reaches for the pad again. "Disconnected?"

"When I lost my temper," I say, "I knew I was throwing stuff. I could see myself doing it, but in my head I didn't *want* to be throwing stuff. It felt like someone else was moving my arms, you know?"

She's writing furiously. "Yes," she says. "I know exactly." Her words are long and drawn out. She's thinking about what she's writing and not so much what she's saying.

"So now what?" I ask. "You're going to tell me that because I lost my mom, I'm going to—what? Hook up with one bad guy after another and get pregnant?"

Dr. Artaud smiles. "That's what I might expect from a girl who lost her *father*, Star," she says. "I expect you to be pissed off."

"Why?"

"You tell me. Who are you mad at, Star?"

"I told you—Farris…"

She leans forward. Her fingers steeple and press against her chin. "Farris was a convenient target. Who are you *mad* at?"

An answer comes to me. It almost slips out, but I catch it before I say it aloud. It's not right, I tell myself. I swallow. My eyes wander to the desktop, to the wall, to the floor. But a voice—my voice—is screaming a name in my head.

I can't hold it in. My lips move, and I say the name in a whisper.

"Yes," says Dr. Artaud. "I understand."

I try to explain what I'm feeling. I'm not picking at the thread or sniffling or hiding behind my hair anymore. I'm talking.

And when Dr. Artaud talks, I listen.

Later, when the session ends, I nod and haul myself to my feet. Dr. Artaud guides me toward the door. I pass through, and I expect to hear it click shut behind me, but instead I hear her calling out to me. "Star?" she says. When I turn, I see her leaning against the doorframe. She takes off her glasses ands rubs her eyes. It's the first time I get the idea that our sessions are as rough on her as they are on me. "The reason you react so…powerfully? It's because you have a strong personality. Emotionally, you're all bone and muscle. That's a good thing."

The moment hangs there. I know I'm supposed to react, to give her something in return for the compliment, but I don't feel anything. I don't feel anything at all.

5
When I Get Home

Dooley won't talk to me.

We're in a purgatory with Sheetrock walls. ISS—in-school suspension. Dooley and I will get to spend two days here. Farris Tidwell turned out to be an even bigger idiot than I had imagined. He went straight to alternative school when Mr. Dunwoodie, the assistant principal, found the can of spray paint in his locker.

I got here five minutes before Dooley did and chose a seat near the back of the room. I left my backpack on the desk next to mine, saving Dooley a spot, and when he finally arrived I waggled a finger at him to say hello. He stopped—he actually looked right at me—then picked a seat four rows away. Now he takes out his art pad and hunches over it, scratching at it first with one kind of pencil then another. His knees press against the desk in front of him. His elbows dig into the desktop. I wait, pretending not to care but glancing at him every few seconds to see if he tosses me a look over his shoulder. Except for the tiny flicking of his wrist as he draws, he doesn't move. An hour passes. I stare at his narrow shoulders, the back of his shaggy head, and one little sliver of an ear.

Pepperland

I've never been in ISS before. The room has no windows, just a tiny pane in the door. Someone, years ago, covered the glass with black paint. When I look closely, I can see little scratches in it, places where students dug at the paint with a car key or bent paper clip to see outside. The fluorescent brightness in the hallway shines through the scratches. A name—Jon—is a little silver light against the black background. I can't stare at it very long, because it makes me sad. A little pile of old magazines sits on the floor in the corner. *Seventeen* and *Glamour* and *Sports Illustrated*. I'm not interested.

Yesterday afternoon my teachers all received a little note telling them I was suspended and reminding them to send along my assignments. Three handouts sit on my desk, untouched. I scribble the words to a Fleetwood Mac song on the outside of my official sophomore "Class of '83" PeeChee folder. The girl next to me writes a note in huge, angry letters I can read from here: *So go with her. Think I care!!??* Someone knocks at the door, a student aide with more assignments. We all look up at her, alerted by the loud click of her suede boots against the linoleum. Then, curiosity satisfied, we look back down. A bell rings, ending first period, but we don't move. The ISS teacher holds a newspaper. Its pages rattle loudly as he turns them.

If I squint just right, the numerals appear to float off the clock face and hover in front of it. I have to stop after a minute, though. Squinting too long gives me a headache. Instead I study the second hand for seven straight minutes. I watch it click at each mark between the numbers, tapping my index finger to keep the rhythm. I now have an acute sense of exactly how long five seconds is. My new talent is almost like having a superpower. From this moment on I can hum a note for five seconds, or hold my breath, or scratch an itch. People can say, do *this* for exactly five seconds, and I'll be able to. Some musicians have perfect pitch; I have perfect time. I'm a stopwatch.

God, I am so bored.

I'm worried about Dooley. I can tell, even from behind, that he's in that little zone he gets into when he's doing his art. Sometimes, when we're watching TV, he'll grab a sheet of notebook paper and start sketching without even thinking about it. After a few moments he just closes off. Like shades over the eyes. Plugs in the ears. The universe is him, the chair he's sitting on, the pencil, and the paper. When he's finished, he looks up at the television and sees that the show is over, or the movie is forty minutes further along than he remembered, and he makes me tell him how the story turned out.

I can't talk to him. I can't signal him. Little gestures, held close to the body, are about all I can get away with here, but he's in front of me. He's *deliberately* in front of me. He planned it that way.

To spite him, I do my work.

At 11:00 they let us into the cafeteria for lunch. Dooley throws together a salad, piling his plate with lettuce and tomato, then smothering the pile with cheese and bacon bits. His arm moves mechanically from the salad bar to his plate. I don't think he's even looking at the food; he's studying the eyes, the nose, the forehead reflecting back at him from the sneeze guard. When he's finished filling his plate, he stares down at it, as if he's not sure where it came from or why he's holding it. I reach for a cheeseburger, Tater Tots, and a banana, and then I follow him to a table.

We sit together, near a wall on which they've painted the

school mascot. A huge snarling grizzly wearing a football uniform stares down at us. Dooley doesn't say anything. I unwrap my burger and tear it into bite-sized pieces with my fingers. Then I stare at the pieces. Dooley jabs at his salad with a plastic fork.

"So why are you mad at me?" I ask.

His fork goes *tick tick tick* against the plate. "Who said I was mad?"

"You picked a desk six miles away from me in ISS. You haven't spoken to me since yesterday. You're not even looking at me now."

He makes a big show of looking at me—full eye contact, no blinking, mouth a straight line, like a villain in one of his comic book drawings. The cuts on his face have scabbed over, and the bruising around his cheekbone has a blue-green tinge. He presses his elbow against his side as if his ribs hurt or he's guarding them.

"You shouldn't have hit Farris," he says.

He barely whispers, but the words are like one of those big steel balls that crash into buildings. A loud *krang* and a cloud of concrete dust. Something inside me crumples. *"What?"*

"You shouldn't have hit him. You should have stayed out of it."

He slides down the bench away from me, and his salad becomes the center of his world. He meditates over it—elbows jammed down on the tabletop, eyes half-lidded, palms pressed against his forehead like he's trying to push something out of his brain. In my mind I see him the way he looked yesterday. I see his eyes, wide and almost…accepting when he saw Farris Tidwell was bent on hurting him. And so I have a brief moment where I tell myself that Dooley is an idiot. He *needed* my help. He needed me to bash Farris in the face, every bit as much as Farris himself needed to be bashed. A friend saved, a bully humbled. Justice and balance restored to the universe. I did exactly the right thing, and I paid for it, willingly, with two days of clock-watching in ISS.

But Dooley, of course, is not an idiot, so I have to ask myself why he would say something so incredibly stupid.

Then it dawns on me. I begin to understand why he's angry, why he won't speak to the girl who took up his battle for him.

"That's it, isn't it," I say.

He won't look at me. His hands come away from his face, crinkle into fists, and deliver two solid knocks to his forehead.

I slide down the bench and lay my hand on his arm, drawing the fist down. "Stop that, okay? You're mad at me for ending the fight, because getting your ass kicked is better than getting help from a girl, is that it? By some weird guy logic, you think I helped Farris prove his point. A girl fights your battles for you, so you must be less of a man, is that it?"

Dooley lets out a little huff of breath that almost sounds like a laugh. "Yeah, well, maybe something like that."

I could just swat him.

Sometimes I wonder if all girls are as muddy and incomprehensible to guys as guys are to me. I don't get guys at all. They defy explanation. I figure that, whatever they do, they do it because they're guys and it's wired into their bones. They can't help it.

I scoot over and give Dooley a hug. "I'm sorry."

He picks up his fork and stares at it. Somehow, in all his earlier jabbing, he's broken off one of the points. "S'awright," he mumbles.

"I'm apologizing, but it's still the stupidest thing I've ever heard."

"Noted," says Dooley.

"So we're okay now?"

"We're fine."

"You're talking to me again?"

"I think so. Yes, that's me. I recognize my voice."

"Okay, then," I say. "Now I'm happy." I can feel all the tension leaving my muscles. My biceps ache as though I've been lifting heavy boxes.

On the table next to Dooley is his art pad, the big one with the heavy wire binding and eleven by seventeen pages. "What are you working on?" In response he flips through several pages, then lets the pad land on the table with a loud *thwap*. Whatever he's drawn, I already know he's proud of it.

"Ooh…" I tell him. "Nice."

It's something like the splash page of a comic book. A muscular man in a T-shirt and jeans bursts through a brick wall. His hair flies, his face snarls, his arm hooks a vicious uppercut. The detail is astonishing. Wrinkles on the man's shirt move with him, veins in his arm pop out, the bones in his hand have form and hardness under the skin. In the foreground a second figure flies out toward the viewer as if struck. His arms flail; his feet leave the ground. Dooley used cross-hatching to give the figure's face an unwashed or unshaven look. The hair appears stringy and dirty. Then I study the figure even more closely, the pudginess around the middle, the roundness to the face, the eyes just a little too close together, and I recognize him. The fat, dirty man flying out of the picture is Farris Tidwell.

And the hero? I see it now—in the face and eyes, if not in the muscles. The hero is Dooley.

☆

I've been thinking a lot about John Lennon the artist. I mean, yes, he's a great musician, but he's also an artist in the same sense Dooley is. Lennon draws, he sketches, he paints. His style is cartoonish and full of squiggly lines.

Once Lennon painted a nude portrait of his wife—an image that apparently bothered everyone but the two of them. John and Yoko appeared naked on the cover of their *Two Virgins* album as well, though most people haven't seen that picture because the album came out in a brown paper wrapper. All I've seen is the wrapper itself, with a little oval cut out to reveal the two faces. Here's my point: Lennon is also naked in his music. Emotionally, I mean. Look at the lyrics to "Help!" or "Nowhere Man." Or get past the Beatles and look at "Jealous Guy" or "Crippled Inside." Not a stitch of clothing anywhere. Dooley is naked in his art, too, only I'm not sure he knows it. Every dream of his, every fantasy, every insecurity gets laid out sooner or later in charcoal pencil or pastel. Give him a few years, and his sketchbooks will be like a thousand-page biography of his life. Just read between the squiggles.

Every intuition tells me that great art, like Dooley's, has to peel away the outer layers, because it's the only way to get to the places where we're all the same.

Right now I'm telling myself that I can be just as open in my own music. I can be like John Lennon. I'm sprawled on my bed, a spiral notebook open in front of me and my chin resting on my fist. I write the word "mother," stare at it, then write over the letters again and again until they look black and ragged. I doodle a cube shape. I doodle a picture of a guitar. Nothing. Before I know it, I've torn the sheet from the notebook and crumpled it, tossing it so that it ricochets off the wall and lands on the carpet with the three others I've discarded.

I breathe, deeply and consciously, and tell myself to start over.

Pepperland

M-O-T-H-E-R.

I make the letters two inches tall this time so the word covers almost the entire sheet of paper. I want it to be in my face, unavoidable. I'm hoping I'll have a burst of inspiration, that the word, staring back at me in those huge letters, will make me think of another word and then another. It doesn't. I'm totally locked.

I draw a line through the word, and my pen starts moving back and forth, scribbling. I must be bearing down harder, too, because the fourth or fifth scribble tears a gash in the paper. I throw the notebook out my bedroom door and watch it skitter down the hallway, its pages flapping.

Syke won't be home for another couple of hours. Nothing on TV. The sun streaming through my window feels warm on my face.

Screw writing the song. I'm going to Dooley's.

Dooley stretches out on his bed, his back against the headboard and his sketchpad braced against his knees. The bed is unmade, and I can pick up just a tiny whiff of body funk from the sheets. The clothes he wore yesterday lie on the floor. When we came in, he hurriedly scooped up the underwear and stuffed it under the pile formed by the shirt and pants. The room is all Dooley. Jimi Hendrix, playing a white Stratocaster left-handed, stares down from a wall poster. A sheet of corkboard covers the opposite wall, and Dooley uses it as a display area for his artwork: delicate pen-and-ink drawings on the back of three by five cards, pencil sketches on typing paper, a painting in watercolor and gouache of Rapunzel spilling waves of red hair down the side of an emerald tower. She moves me the most: Rapunzel is in a prison of sorts, but it's a lovely prison. The air around her seems to glisten, the vines crawling along the tower are magical, the tumbling hair is beautiful and hints at escape.

"Time?" says Dooley.

I've been sitting on the floor, plunking in curiosity at his bass guitar. I hate it, though. The fingerboard is too long for my arm and too wide for my hand. The strings feel like cable against my fingertips. I put it down and check my watch. "Five minutes."

Tonight a local station is airing *The Wizard of Oz* as some kind of fall special event. It's special because they are airing it *without commercials,* which means Dooley can finally perform an experiment whispered about by Pink Floyd fans. He tosses aside his art pad and rushes to turn on the television. "Grab the tape, okay?"

It's already in my hand. The cover is glossy black, and in the center is a large pyramid shape. A beam of white light strikes the pyramid, then escapes through the other side as a rainbow spray.

"See?" he says. "It starts out black and white, then turns to color."

"Yeah, yeah, I get it." The rumor started that *The Dark Side of the Moon* works as an eerie sort of soundtrack to *The Wizard of Oz.* Dooley's been dying to test the idea.

We watch, munching slices of bologna and cheese we've stuck between soda crackers. "This is cool beyond cool," says Dooley. The thrill lasts maybe forty minutes. After that we've forgotten the movie, and we're looking for more food and better entertainment. I make chocolate chip cookies that turn out flat and crunchy and black on the bottom. We eat them anyway, then warm up a can of ravioli Dooley's found in back of the kitchen cupboard. Dooley tries to work out a bass line to a song but gives up after five minutes, tossing his bass onto the bed. He plops down next to it, his eyes finding the TV screen. Dorothy mouths her lines silently.

I haul myself to my feet. I gather paper plates, pluck cookie crumbs from the carpet, stack Dixie cups. Dooley just stares ahead. He's slipped into one of his silences. I know him, and I know what these moments mean. Dooley likes to build a little tent around himself, paint a problem on the inside walls, and stare at it. That's what he's doing now. There's no point in talking to him. Whatever he's thinking, I'll squeeze it out of him later.

The silence feels weird, so I give his knee a nudge. "Come on," I say. "You better take me home."

We escape just as his mother arrives, passing her on the stairs leading to the apartment. She wears a red uniform, a plastic nametag, and a hairnet, and she gives me a wary nod when she sees me. Norah O'Doul manages a pizza place a few miles from here and rarely gets home before nine o'clock. Though it's fairly cold out, she carries her shoes in her hand and pauses to massage one foot.

"Don't be late," she says to Dooley. It feels more like a plea than an order.

"I won't."

"Did you clean the kitchen?" she asks. I cringe, remembering the cracker box and the empty wrappers from the cheese slices.

"I will when I get back."

I expect an argument, but she's too tired. Dooley and I turn away, and she stays there on the staircase, swaying on one foot, fingers squeezing cramps out of the toes of the other.

When I Get Home

I'm home in ten minutes. Dooley parks his Gremlin in the driveway next to Syke's truck and leaves the engine running. He stares forward, and his fingers shift around as he grips the steering wheel, making a little squeak. When he finally turns toward me, he leans in a little too close. Then it all gets crazy. I feel his hands, these huge bony hands, land on either side of my face and pull me toward him. His lips press against mine, but the kiss is clumsy and hard. It hurts. His mouth moves back and forth, and he says "Mmmmmmmm," which makes his lips vibrate. I can feel my teeth scraping the inside of my mouth. I make a sound like someone choking on water and try to pull back, but his hands have me locked in. I have to push against his shoulders—*hard*—and draw my head back before he understands. *Stop!*

I'm staring at him, my mouth open and my fingers touching my lips. They feel a little puffy. Dooley pulls away as far as he can go, his shoulder pressing into the door. He squeezes his eyes shut and bangs his head a couple of times against the window glass.

"I'm sorry," he says. "I'm so sorry…"

"Stop doing that," I say. "Stop hitting your head. What were you *thinking?*"

"I wasn't… I'm sorry…"

His head lolls against the window. He still hasn't opened his eyes.

"Dooley…"

I could go on. I could insist that we sit here until he explains himself, but I need to get out of this car right now. I'm in no mood to listen. Better that we separate—get alone, get quiet, get rested, and think.

"I'm going in," I say. "Go home. Don't call me. We'll talk tomorrow."

I grab the handle and punch my shoulder against the door to open it. I want to make a dash for the house, but then I remember I went to Dooley's with all my school stuff. I have to push the stupid seat forward and reach around for my backpack. His dome light doesn't work; I'm fiddling in the dark, grabbing at shadows, at seatbelts.

"Star?"

His voice is barely louder than the sound of the television inside my house. I ignore him at first. My hand lands on the backpack, and I yank on it. It slaps me in the stomach. I slam the door and turn.

"Star?"

Dooley hasn't moved. It's like he's squeezing himself into the smallest space his body will allow. I hug my backpack and wait.

"I have to tell you something," Dooley says. "Farris. What he said—what he painted on my locker?"

I nod.

"I'm not, okay? I'm not what he said I was."

I'm too jumbled up inside to know how to answer. I wait too long, and my hesitation gives him the wrong idea.

"*Really.*"

"Okay," I tell him.

He relaxes, sinking into his seat. His long arms unfold like scissors; one hand grabs the steering wheel while the other puts the car in gear. He smiles weakly. I step back and watch him roll out of the driveway. Still smiling, he hangs one arm outside the window and waves good-bye.

6

Instant Karma

He's coming.

I heard it on the radio. The announcer tossed off the news like it was nothing—a sale on shoes at J.C. Penney's, a new sandwich at Jack in the Box...

I haven't touched the Lennon letter since the day I found it. It leans against the mirror over my table. When I'm getting ready in the morning, the little fishlike paisley shapes on the envelope shine brightly under my lamp. I try not to notice them. At night, when I'm lying in bed like I am right now, a little moonlight spills in through the window and turns the walls and furniture blue. When this happens, the fishlike shapes fade to gray and black. Swirling around them is my mother's handwriting, looking like a curly thread someone has dropped across the paper.

He's coming. He's coming *here*. I have to think about this.

I came home from school today on the bus just like I always do. I vacuumed, I dusted, I made dinner, I did my homework—just like I always do. And as I worked, I turned on the little kitchen radio, and I heard a song I hadn't heard before. I remember it started with three chimes—*pling...pling...pling*—followed by three beats of silence. I thought of those little

cymbals on the fingers of gypsy dancers. Then voice and guitar came in, just those two instruments, and I felt like I was listening to someone singing and playing in a chair just a few
feet away.

A minute into the song I knew I was listening to John
Lennon. He was singing about starting over. Starting over in
love, starting over in life, starting over in music. I put down
my dishcloth and sat on the floor. Later, when Syke wandered
in and asked me what I was doing, I realized the song was
over and I was still sitting there hugging my knees.

So now I'm lying in bed, and moonlight is spilling through
the window, and the black loops of my mother's handwriting
sit five feet away, and I have to think about all this. Because
after the song finished, a DJ announced that Lennon had a
new album coming out on November 15, which is next
Tuesday. He said that Elton John was appearing in concert at
the L.A. Concert Pavilion the week after the release, and
rumor had it that Lennon might be a surprise guest at the
show.

He's coming. Think. Think. Think.

My phone rings, and I jump at the noise. The little clock on
my bed table says 11:15, so I know who's calling. I let it ring
two more times while I decide whether or not to pick up. I
finally surrender.

"Hey."

"Hey," he says, "have you heard it yet?"

He knows already. "Once," I tell him. "On KMET."

"You should have listened to KLOS. They played it three
times."

I don't really know what to say, so I say nothing. I hear
Dooley sniffle once, then clear his throat. We haven't spoken
since the weird kiss last night. Today was busy, hectic at

school, and I would have had to go out of my way a little to run into him. I didn't. I'm not really mad; I've just been... startled...for the last twenty-four hours. In my mind I can still feel the roughness of the kiss, and I wonder about it. Part of me worries, while another part thinks I should write off the roughness as just a strange collision of the moment: my shock mixed with his clumsiness.

"So are you going to the Elton John show?" he asks.

"Yes," I tell him. Then: "I think so. I'm not sure."

"Are you aware that you just covered every possible answer except a definite 'no'?"

"Dooley, I'm thinking about it."

Another pause. Our conversations are never this strained. Neither one of us ever chatters, and we've shared lots of comfortable silences. This isn't one of them. I know he's going to wait to talk about what happened until he's sure I won't get mad at him again. That's the problem with having a temper— especially *my* kind of temper. It puts off a lot of good conversations.

I try to lighten things up, make the water flow a little more smoothly between us. Dooley is a walking encyclopedia of music information. "Hey," I say, "trivia question. This has been bothering me for days. John Lennon wrote a song for his mother—"

"'Julia,'" he says. "1968. The White Album. Two-record set. It's the last song on the B side of the first record."

I laugh at the thorough answer. He's trying so hard. "Not that one. This song came later, after the Beatles broke up."

"Oohhh, yeah yeah yeah," he says. "Riiiight...it's on the *Plastic Ono Band* album."

"Do you know the title?"

"Sure," he says. "It's called 'Mother'."

"Okay—right," I say. "That's the one. Is it kind of a soft guitar piece?"

"Nah," says Dooley. "Lennon screams it. He screams the whole song."

☆

Memories of my mother play like old home movies. The images are large, vibrant, and I have this sensation that the flat surface on which they're projected would ripple underneath my hand if I were to reach out and touch them.

Like right now.

I hear my mother in the living room, snapping the latches of her guitar case. The sound calls me like the grind of a can opener calls a cat. I follow it out from the kitchen, where I've been licking my fingers after dipping them into the jar of strawberry jam. The jar still sits on the floor in front of the refrigerator. The lid has rolled off somewhere, maybe under the table or behind the trash can. I wasn't paying attention. I wipe my hand against my pajamas, and it sticks. I can see that my fingers shine, and they're faintly pink.

I am five years old.

I find my mother just as she lifts the guitar from its case. It's an old, round-shouldered Gibson acoustic with a sunburst finish. I like the way the black lightens to a dark gold around the sound hole. I also like the little plastic knobs on the front, which Mom lets me twirl while she's playing. Mostly I like the sound the guitar makes, the way the strings keep singing after she strikes a chord. Sometimes she lets me run my own fingers across them, and I hit the strings hard, just to hear the sound go on and on and on.

Mom has a sheet of paper in front of her. She's written down the words to a song and the chords that go with them.

Instant Karma

She strums once, hums a note, and starts singing, looking at the fingerboard as she plays. Her long, curly hair spills over her shoulders and covers her face. She has to shake her head to keep it back, and I like to watch her do that, too. My hair is only as long as my chin, but I shake my head along with her.

The song is "Across the Universe," and she sings it terribly. She misses chord changes, loses a beat here and there. Strings buzz when she doesn't press down hard enough. She closes her eyes and sings loudly, smiling all the while. I shriek *la la la*'s with her. Together we make pure, nerve-rattling noise, and it's wonderful. I jump up and down to the beat and just know that I'm dancing. Mom smiles and sings, going flat at the end of the refrain. I'm filled. Something is bursting inside me. I twirl, my arms outstretched. I'm a pop star. For a five year old, the words of the refrain are a perfect reflection of life and love and security. My mother is singing at the top of her lungs. Her eyes are closed, and she's smiling. I dance and spin around her until I'm dizzy and my legs collapse beneath me. When she gets to the end, I know the refrain well enough to sing along.

Nothing's gonna change my world...
Nothing's gonna change my world...

I don't know why these images come to me so vividly. The truth is, I have very few memories of my mother playing guitar. The old Gibson she had vanished around the time she married Syke. My head works strangely, though. Sometimes I'll close my eyes, or open my closet door, or just look down at some food on my plate, and something will come back to me. I'll open the bathroom cabinet and see her dipping some tweezers in peroxide and using them to pull a splinter from my finger. It's more than memory, though. The harsh peroxide burns my nostrils, and I see the dirt under my fingernails and the scratch on my hand where I scraped the wood fence. I feel the splinter tugging at my skin before it pops out, the sting of the Merthiolate she dabs on afterward. Most vividly, I feel the press of her lips against my forehead when she's finished and the warm, waxy feel of her lipstick.

What hurts is that these memories come only when *they* want. I have trouble commanding them. I have photographs of my mother, from all stages of her life, scattered here and there in my room and around the house: Mom at her college graduation, Mom at her wedding to Syke, Mom on horseback, Mom with a broken arm, her cast covered with get-well scribblings. I look at these pictures every day, because my greatest fear—the possibility that truly terrifies me—is that I'll start to forget what she looked like. I'll see the wedding photo in my mind, every swirl of lace in the gown and veil, but her face will be a blur.

It's been about an hour since Dooley called, and I've been lying awake, listening to a moth flutter against my window screen. The memory of my mother is so fresh and so intense, I feel a powerful warmth mixed with my sadness. I'm smiling, and I close my eyes and cover the smile with my hands as though I can hold onto it.

It strikes me that, at this moment, with my mother so close, I should be able to write the perfect song. I crawl out from my bed and reach for the Telecaster. I keep it in the corner of my room, balanced on a guitar stand, and my hand finds it quickly even in the dark. I take it back to the bed with me and sit with it in my lap. I strum a G chord. I strum a D. The strings are light and jangly and quiet, like I'm fingering rubber bands. But the sound of the chords is too simple, too folky. I try minors—C-sharp minor and F-sharp minor, an E chord to brighten it all—but the tone is too sad. Sevenths, I find, are too bluesy for what my ear wants; major sevenths are too elegant. I pick through a series of odd jazz chords, ninths and elevenths and augmented, the harmonies so different in some of them that I'm not sure of the names. They lose me. They're complex and full of nuance, but I can't feel anything in them. They seem cold. I'm trying to write a song for my mother. I'm looking for chords that wear blue jeans and keep their hair in a ponytail, and I can't find them.

I have another idea: Try lyrics first. Put thoughts on paper. Get a picture of my mother in my head and write down what I see. I lay the guitar down on the sheets next to me and reach for my pen and my journal. Smiling, I close my eyes and think of my mom, and—

Clang.

The door slams shut in my face. The feelings disappear. All the warmth I was experiencing, all the closeness, flows out of me like someone's overturned a glass. I know this feeling. I've felt it before many times, and I know what it means. I won't be writing a song for my mother tonight.

When I was in grade school, kids played a cruel game called Keep Away. You'd grab someone's book or whatever and toss it to a friend. The poor fool who wanted his book back would chase after it, only to see it arc over his head. The "fun" was in the humiliation the victim felt as he or she ran one way and then the other, always getting close but never quite getting a hand back on the book.

That's me right now. My muses love to torture me.

I wonder what my mother ever did with that old Gibson. I'm sure I would have remembered if it had been lost or stolen, and I can't recall her ever selling it. It just sort of disappeared from her life. She married Syke, got a better job, and didn't have time to play it anymore, I suppose.

Which means it's probably still around here somewhere.

The idea makes my insides jangle. I crawl out of bed again and put on my slippers. They're a little old and stretched out, so I make tiny *shuff-flip shuff-flip* noises as I walk down the hall and into the kitchen. From here I can sneak right into the garage. I open the door, my hand finds the switch, and the whole garage brightens like the inside of a department store. Syke sometimes likes to work on his Harley after dark, so he installed fluorescent fixtures in the ceiling.

I don't know why I'm expecting to find anything. I've been in the garage hundreds of times, and I've never seen that guitar. Dooley and I wrestled with the boxes just a few days ago. I know it's not here. Still, I wander around, stare at the boxes we never opened, look in all the corners I usually ignore. The boxes I see are cubes—the wrong size and shape for a guitar. I don't see a guitar case. I don't see a spot where my mother could have hidden one. *This was a stupid idea,* I tell myself. *You have school tomorrow. Go back to bed.*

I head toward the door, and I'm about to shut off the light, when I glance up at some sheets of plywood lying across the beams. A few years ago Syke slid them up there to keep them flat. Knowing my mom as I do, she would think that's a perfect place to store stuff she was tired of looking at. I grab a flashlight from Syke's workbench and haul the ladder away from the wall. Mom would laugh if she could see me. The ladder isn't heavy, but it's tall and it teeters as I try to hold it. I have to drag it around the Harley—God help me if I drop it there!—and bring it closer to the plywood sheets. I've got the flashlight pinned in my armpit, and I'm holding the stupid ladder straight, trying to kick the legs apart. Finally I've got it standing on its own. I climb up four, five rungs. From here I can just peek over the top of the plywood. The lights hang about eight inches below where I'm looking, so I click on the flashlight.

I see an old beach pail, a little plastic shovel sticking out of it, crusted with sand. I see a box of Christmas decorations and a rusty chainsaw with a broken chain. Behind these is a black shape.

I stop breathing.

When I shine the light on it, I can see it's a guitar case. I have to move up a step on the ladder to reach it. I push the chainsaw to one side. When I lean forward, my fingers can just reach around the handle, and I drag the case toward me. Dust on the plywood puffs up in my face and makes me cough.

It's not easy to climb down a ladder while holding a guitar, but I've had enough practice at the lifeguard stand to pull it off. I set down the case, wrestle the ladder back to its place against the wall, and leave Syke's flashlight *exactly* where I found it. The guitar case is filthy, but I hug it against me anyway and carry it into the house.

I spend five minutes wiping it down. The damp cloth turns the dust to mud, so I rinse the cloth and keep wiping. I have to do this again and again. As the dust comes off, I find that I'm wiping more and more slowly. I'm *rubbing* the cloth over the case—a case that is already clean. I tell myself I'm done, but my hand is still working. Finally I do what I *really* want to do: give in to impulse. I set the cloth aside and let my bare fingers move across the case. It's cold to the touch, the surface rough and pebbled, and I like the feel of it.

I lug the case into my room and lay it across my bed. The latches are gold-colored and speckled with rust, and I let my thumb flip one. It clicks up like a light switch and stays. I see a smudge of fingerprint and wonder if it's mine. The thought occurs to me that it might be my mother's, and I feel a little chill.

I pop two more latches.

The last latch is near the headstock. This one I raise slowly, lifting it with my thumb and guiding it upward until I hear a little snap. Sometimes I can touch one of my mom's hats, a blouse, a piece of jewelry, and not feel anything other than *this would look good with my skirt.* Other times I feel a jolt, a little shot of electricity in the tips of my fingers—almost as though the object has some of my mother's life attached to it.

I have a memory of sitting in my mother's lap as she showed me how to tie my shoes. I was leaning into her, smelling the shampoo she'd used in her hair and the fabric softener in her blouse. Her arms were wrapped around me, and our cheeks were touching. She was whispering directions, and I could feel her breath tickling my ear. "Make a loop like this..." she said, "and then take the other lace..."

So now, when I hold something of my mom's, and when I'm especially lucky, I feel just as I did at the moment I first tied my shoes: Warm, safe, the sounds and smells and touches of my mother wrapped all around me. I'm having one of those moments as I flip the last latch, and I close my eyes and enjoy it for a few seconds.

When I lift the lid of the case and peer inside, the instrument looks just like I remember—the dark wood on the face of it, and the way it lightens to gold in the center. I see fine cracks in the finish, like someone's laid a spiderweb across it. It's not until the lid flips over completely that I notice something is wrong. I slip the guitar from the case, and its insides rattle. I hear wood rubbing on wood. The strings sag against the fingerboard, and the neck jiggles in my hand. I see a crack along the seam where the top meets the body.

Instant Karma

The guitar is in *pieces*. I want to cry, I'm so disappointed, but then I tell myself that an old guitar is nothing to cry over. I know from experience that you spend your tears on the big hurts, not the little day-to-day jabs. *It was a beat-up thing anyway,* I tell myself. *And you already have another guitar.*

I lay the instrument back in its case and put everything on the floor, leaving the lid open so I can see inside. I can't imagine what could have damaged it so badly. Staring at the wounded guitar, I have an odd feeling that I'm supposed to understand something here, but I'm clueless as to what the message might be. I close the guitar case with a nudge from my big toe.

I'm drawn again to the envelope on my makeup table. This time it's as if a pair of hands presses against my back and pushes me across the room. A moment later the envelope is in my hand. I see my mother's handwriting, I see John Lennon's name, and the phrase that was ringing in my head earlier comes back to me: *He's coming. He's coming here.* Mom put a stamp on the envelope but left an inch of space for another. In 1964 she couldn't find John Lennon's address and so never knew how much postage she needed. Five cents or ten? England or America? The letter, never mailed, ended up in the back pages of her old yearbook.

And from there into my hand.

I know now that tonight is all about unfinished business. Not so much my mother's as my own. Tonight—seeing Mom's old guitar, holding this envelope—I can feel the truth in what Dr. Artaud says. I have to write a song for my mother...for *me*. Unfinished business. And the way I'll succeed—and I know this the same way I know my heart is beating and my lungs are drawing in air—is that I'll compose it on my mother's guitar.

And one more thing....

Pepperland

I'm going to deliver my mother's letter. I'm not sure how, but I'm going to put it into John Lennon's hand myself, and I'm going to tell him how my mother played his songs for me and how she sang terribly and how I danced. Then I'll whisper to him that my mother died, and I'll say, "Tell me about Julia."

And he will.

In my mind, I see a huge, flat piece of rock in the middle of my chest. A finger points at that rock, and lightning shoots from the finger. The lightning carves words in the stone. I'm that serious.

I set the envelope down and once again open the guitar case. I lift the guitar, juggling pieces that seem to be held together only by the loose wire strings, and I try to imagine the instrument whole again. I try to see it the way it was when my mother played, filled with that singing sound it made when she formed a chord and I dragged my hand across the strings.

In the middle of all these thoughts, the strap button pops off the body and clatters to the floor.

I'm going to need some help.

7

Fixing a Hole

I find Dooley under the oak tree at school. When I step off the bus, I see him as I see him every morning—seated on the edge of the brick planter, his eyes focused on some work in his lap. Really, the planter is too low for a chair, so his legs form a sharp, inverted V, with his knobby knees as the point. His arms are the same way, long lines with sharp bends in the middle.

I'm walking toward him from maybe ten feet away, holding a very large guitar case in my hand, and so far he hasn't noticed me. I just get the hunched shoulders, downturned face, and haystack hair. Then something reaches him. It may be the noise of all the other students walking past, or the loud punch of the bus's parking brake as the driver releases it. Whatever it was that broke through, Dooley looks up and finds me. He's been tearing a sheet of paper from his art pad, but now he freezes. Part of the paper is still in the pad, part of it is torn out, and a breeze whips one corner. He doesn't move. Seconds pass; he's still looking at me and holding the paper between his thumb and forefinger. I walk over and sit next to him. He seems to take this as permission to continue his work. His shoulders relax, and he finishes tearing the sheet.

Pepperland

We sit together, silent. I watch him fold the paper in half and turn down the corners. I recognize these moves as the first two steps in the making of another pterodactyl airplane. We don't have to talk, at least not at this moment, so I become an audience. I really don't mind. I like to watch Dooley work. He folds paper with the same precision I find in his drawings. Right now, for example, I can see him measuring with his eye. He's made the first of the wing folds, and now he wants to be sure the opposite wing sticks out at the same angle. It does, but only because Dooley forces it to out of sheer artistic instinct. I find myself nodding during the effort and smiling at the success. I watch him continue his work, memorizing each step as he completes it, following his fingers as he pinches a fold and draws his thumb and forefinger along its length. The pterodactyl takes shape.

"Are you mad at me?" he asks.

Wow. I perk up at this. So, he *has* been thinking about the other night. I still remember the look on his face when he waved good-bye, like we were George and Emily in *Our Town*, just coming back from the malt shop. I'm not sure what felt stranger, the situation or the fact that he was just his typical dorky self afterward.

"I'm not mad," I tell him. "You just caught me off guard."

"Sorry," he says—and continues folding.

Three narrow pink lines cross Dooley's cheekbone. They're the last I can see of his fight with Farris. When he turns from the sun, they're barely visible, and it's as if something small and far away is casting a faint light on his face. But now he looks toward me, into the light, and the marks stand out—perfectly parallel, lighter than his skin, and glistening. Dooley still coats them with some kind of ointment.

Now he sits there staring, giving me the strangest look: mouth slightly open, eyes not quite on my face, like he can't bring himself to look at me. He's studying my ear, or some imaginary bird on my left shoulder.

"So what was it about?" I ask. "The kiss, I mean. You've never done that before."

He turns back to his folding. "I dunno. Guess I just felt like kissing you. Sorry if it was a *problem*."

"Well, there you go," I say, throwing up my hands. "You *felt* like it. Silly me, that I didn't see that before."

Oddly enough, I hadn't ever thought of Dooley as a possible boyfriend. We met last school year when my mom was sick, and then came all the funeral planning and the interviews with therapists and life wasn't so much fun anymore. I had room for maybe a dozen items on my list of things to think about, and frankly, guys didn't make the cut. Dooley was just kind of there. I could cry in front of him without feeling stupid. I could be quiet and sullen, sometimes even mean, and it didn't seem to bother him. And if I felt guilty and apologized, he seemed genuinely taken aback, as though it hadn't occurred to him to be offended by my bad behavior.

This sounds terrible, but I suppose I also never thought of Dooley as a possible boyfriend because—well—he's not much to look at. He's tall, but in a gangly, giraffe sort of way. He walks fast and leads with his head, so that watching him gives me this slightly uncomfortable sense that he's tipping forward. And his nose is a little too rounded and a little too big.

I know how shallow I sound, but I haven't finished making my point. I'm saying I never had romantic feelings for Dooley, but I never wrote him off either. Every now and then, in the middle of the worst days of my life, I could see how decent he was, and how kind. I've always respected his talent, and I even liked the way his mind kept leaping ahead so I was never sure if he was listening to me or thinking about the conversation we'd be having three minutes later. Dooley is like a ring with a pretty stone in the center. After you wear it a while, you don't feel it rubbing against your knuckle or pinching the finger next to it. It's just sitting there on your hand, invisible until that second when light hits the stone and your eye picks up the flare of color. Then you wonder why you never noticed before how special it is.

So no, I never thought of Dooley as a boyfriend.

And yes, I know I could do a whole lot worse. In fact, the idea is starting to feel pretty darn...*interesting*.

"Listen—" I say, and I stop right there.

I don't know how to be subtle around guys. I see other girls pull it off, do the little smile and the hair flip, send the message you like the guy without really saying so. I just never got any good at it. My experience tells me that subtlety is lost on most guys anyway. A brick works well.

"Were you thinking you might want to try again sometime?" I ask.

The paper pterodactyl rattles in Dooley's hand. His eyes widen, and his mouth kind of opens and closes a little. I lean forward and, thankfully, catch him when it's closed. Our lips touch, just a simple puckered-up smack, then I draw away.

Dooley stares at me. I don't think he's figured out yet that he's been kissed.

The bell rings, sending us to first period. He takes his airplane and folds the tip of the left wing so that it points straight up. The tip of the right wing he folds down, so the whole bird looks cockeyed. The angles are all wrong.

When he heaves it into the air, it shoots through a series of barrel rolls and disappears behind the building.

☆

Fixing a Hole

Dooley doesn't hide his emotions well. He wears them on his face and in the way he tilts his head or runs his hand through his hair. You can't help but read what he's feeling, no matter how much you might want to pretend you don't. Later that day I'm standing by my locker, and I see Dooley coming down the hallway. When he's focused, he walks with his head tilted toward the linoleum. His feet take big strides, pushing forward. I don't have a clue how he avoids running into walls or doors. In seconds he's just a few steps away, and he does a little skip, sliding the last two feet so he's standing next to me.

And he's *smiling*.

Now I know something strange and wonderful has happened. Dooley's smile, as I've experienced it, is little more than a curl to one side of his mouth. It suits his basically cynical nature. It says *The world is ridiculous, and often cruel, and aren't you a fool for not seeing it.* Now, though, he shows all his teeth, including the chipped one down in front, and his cheeks have a reddish glow.

"Dooley?"

"Look," he says. He's juggling his art pad and a stack of books in one arm, but a folded sheet of paper dangles from his free hand. He shakes it, and the paper opens. "I just found out."

I see a gorgeous black-and-white picture that looks familiar, but I can't place it. Then I realize that it's a photo reproduction of one of Dooley's pencil sketches: the male gymnast whipping around parallel bars. Huge letters at the top of the flier say *Spectrum Gallery 7th Annual Student Art Exhibition.* Then below that, in slightly smaller letters, I see the words *Gold Medal Winner.* Tucked behind the award notice is a letter printed on Spectrum Gallery stationery. It begins *Dear Mr. O'Doul, Congratulations!* I feel a flush across my neck and chest that prevents me from reading any further.

"Dooley, that's amazing!" I throw my arms around him, and it's like hugging a tree. His bones freeze up.

"Yeah," he says, extricating himself. "Art students from all over the state submitted pieces, but I guess the judges liked mine."

"You guess?" I'm always amazed by Dooley's inability to say anything positive about himself. When something really good happens to him, something he's earned and deserves, he has to leave open the possibility that someone goofed. "What do you win?"

He stares at the floor again. "Um, it means I get a thousand-dollar scholarship to any art school of my choice, and the gallery will show six of my pieces when they open up their new exhibition in a few weeks."

"*Dooley!*"

This news is worth another hug. He's better prepared this time, so he even hugs me back a little.

"What are we going to do to celebrate?" I ask. "Big party? With a band? Oh, the hell with it. Let's call the surviving members of Led Zeppelin and tell them to get their asses back together for a reunion show in my front yard."

He shrugs, which is just the answer I expect.

"Frozen yogurt after school, then," I say. "On me. You can even order the large, if you don't ask for sprinkles."

"Fair enough," he says.

I circle my arm in his and drag him down the hallway, in the general direction of his next class. "Listen," I say, "remember that beat-up guitar case I had with me this morning?"

"Yeah…"

"Well, I need to ask you a big favor."

☆

Fixing a Hole

I didn't tell Dooley about my mission. I told him that I needed to get my mother's guitar fixed, and that I needed him to drive me somewhere after school, but I said nothing about the finger with the lightning and the words burned into the stone. I figure I make him nervous enough already.

I meet him in the parking lot after school, the case containing my mother's Gibson standing upright, my arms wrapped around it. Dooley's Gremlin is like a station wagon, only smaller. It has just two doors—the hatchback lock having long ago rusted shut—so we have to wrestle the guitar case past the seat. Dooley holds my door for me. It makes a loud, metallic pop as he tries to close it.

"Do you know where we're going?" he asks.

"I have directions."

The directions take us five miles straight down Harbor Boulevard. But then they force us to zigzag through a lot of crazy turns and onto a curving road that handles only one-way traffic. I'm beginning to distrust them. We figured twenty-five minutes for this trip, and I know we've been driving for forty.

"You know what?" Dooley asks. "This trip is starting to feel like a scene in one of those Mafia movies. You know, when the big don is riding along in his limo, paying no attention. Then he looks up and says, 'Wait, we passed the restaurant two blocks ago...and who are you? Where's my regular driver Tony?'"

I laugh. He's right. All the buildings look run-down and unfamiliar—and a little threatening with their faded signs and chipped paint. A horn beeps. A Trans Am tears out from behind us. The owner flips us the bird as he passes.

"What was that about?" I ask.

"I slowed down to read the street sign," says Dooley.

Pepperland

"Wait, there it is!"

I can see the place. Above the storefront is a mural, a cowboy seated at a campfire strumming a guitar. The guitar has Band-Aids on its face and a thermometer sticking out of the sound hole. The words *Seegar's Guitar Repair* appear in the painted sky above the cowboy's head.

I'm unbuckled and grabbing for Mom's wounded guitar before Dooley has finished parking.

A little *zing-zing* bell, like one on a bicycle's handlebars, goes off when we walk through the door. The place is small, far smaller than I had imagined, with worn, light brown carpet and wallpaper with pastel stripes every foot or so. I can see where it's peeling up in the corners. A loud hum comes from behind the counter, and from somewhere in the back I hear the rattle of plastic sheeting. A few guitars hang from hooks. The names are familiar to me, even though I don't play an acoustic. I see another Gibson, a Takamine, a Washburn, and several Martins. One has no logo at all on the headstock and is maybe two-thirds the size of my mother's big dreadnought. A delicate, leafy vine, etched in mother-of-pearl, crawls up the entire length of the fingerboard. I trace it with my thumb.

"Can I help you?"

The woman's voice startles me. She's tall and has frizzy, carrot-colored hair that tumbles past her shoulders. Her face is roundish, the skin a little lighter than mine and dotted everywhere with dark brown freckles.

I still have my hand on the pretty guitar with the snaking vine. "This is beautiful," I say.

"Thank you."

"You made it?" I ask.

She just smiles, but the smile radiates pride. I like her.

"It's so small," says Dooley.

"It's a parlor guitar," she explains. "A hundred years ago every home had a little room for visitors, a parlor, where young men would come 'a-courtin' their ladies,' you might say. The rooms were usually pretty small. Families would put in a chair, a loveseat, maybe a spinet piano, and a little guitar." Her eyes finally land on the battered case I'm carrying. "What have you got there?"

I set the case on the counter. She pops the latches and slowly lifts out the pieces of what used to be my mother's guitar. She jiggles the neck. Something rattles inside the body. The face of the guitar dips inward toward the center, like a pillow where a cat's been sleeping. The strings give out a rubbery twang. "Dear God," she asks, "what have you done to this poor thing?"

I feel my face heat up. "It was left up in a garage," I tell her. Even to me, the answer sounds stupid.

The woman studies the dovetail joint where the neck meets the body. Her finger runs along the gaping crack where the top and sides join. She shakes her head. "You can't treat a guitar that way."

"It's my mother's guitar," I explain.

"Well, tell your mom to quit leaving it in the garage."

"She died."

The woman looks up from the guitar, studies my face for a few moments. "I'm sorry," she says. "Mine died a couple of years ago."

I nod.

She offers a handshake. "Teri Seegar."

Her hand is very warm and dry, and the tiny hairs on her forearm are coated in sawdust. For some reason, this little fact makes me like her even more. "I'm Star Cochran. And this is Dooley."

She and Dooley shake hands as well, then Teri removes an object from the pocket of the canvas apron she's wearing. It looks like a rearview mirror from a car, only much smaller, and it's attached to what appears to be a gold pen. She tugs on the mirror, and the pen telescopes out to about eighteen inches. She feeds the mirror through the sound hole, shines a penlight in behind it. "Let's have a look," she says.

I lean forward. Beneath the top of the guitar, I see thin, narrow strips of wood lying across each other, forming an X. Two are cracked. One has split completely. Part of it remains glued to the top; the other part lies loose inside the body of the guitar. It's what I heard rattling. "Those are your braces," Teri says. "They keep the top from cracking under the tension from the strings."

"Why's the guitar falling apart?" I ask.

She lays the mirror down and brushes the sawdust from her arms. "California's a desert, hon. No humidity. The air sucks all the moisture out of a guitar. The wood shrinks. You get a web of cracks across the guitar, what we call finish checking; the joints pull apart. Look over here, Star." She points to a spot behind the counter. Again I notice the humming sound. It's all around me. Near Teri Seegar's feet is a metal box with vents on each side—an industrial humidifier, pumping moisture into the dry air.

"Can you fix the guitar?" I ask.

"Oh, I can fix it," she says. "It's just going to be expensive. I'll need to reglue the x-braces, repair the crack in the top, reset the neck—you're looking at close to five hundred dollars."

This last part is a knife in the chest. I have a little savings account I've cobbled together from baby-sitting—three hundred and seventeen dollars and twelve cents—and ten bucks in my pocket. I can't really ask Syke for help. Without the income my mom pulled in, he's strapped just making the house payment and taking care of the bills. Everything gets paid; we just don't have a lot left over.

Teri Seegar sees what I'm thinking, reading it all in my face. "Look, Star," she says quietly. "You don't have to make a decision now. Leave the guitar here. Let the wood rehumidify. We'll take another look at it then and see if it's worth saving."

Five hundred dollars. If it were five thousand, or fifty thousand, the situation would be the same. But what can I do? I just nod.

Teri Seegar smiles a close-mouthed smile, full of pity. "Come back in a week," she says.

8

The Ballad of
John and Yoko

No one told John Lennon that he couldn't put an end to the Vietnam War.

Politics were never a huge presence in Beatles music. The Beatles started out as mopheads singing "Love Me Do" and "Please Please Me" and "I Saw Her Standing There," but even then, behind the bluesy chord structures and three-part harmonies, you could hear the edge. *That* was Lennon. While McCartney was writing "Yesterday," Lennon was writing "Help!" While McCartney was writing "Ob-La-Di, Ob-La-Da," Lennon was writing "Revolution" and "Happiness Is a Warm Gun." I've seen footage of John Lennon and his wife at their "bed-in," one of those arty events they staged to protest the war. They rented a hotel room, slipped into their pj's, and invited all the media types to come in and meet with them. I guess that after the *Two Virgins* cover, most reporters rushed over thinking they might see something kinky. I can only imagine how surprised and disappointed they must have been to find Lennon and Ono sitting up in bed, discussing Vietnam. They had a crowd of people around them, some with bongos, some with tambourines. Timothy Leary, the Turn On, Tune In, and Drop Out guy, sat cross-legged over in a corner.

The Ballad of John and Yoko

Lennon had his guitar and started riffing verses to "Give Peace a Chance."

Another time Lennon and Ono, hidden in a huge fabric bag, ate chocolate cake and chatted with reporters about the war. When asked what the bag was about, Lennon explained that he wanted the dialogue with reporters to be about issues, about peace, not about what he was wearing or how tired he looked or how long his hair had gotten.

"How long *is* your hair?" a reporter asked snidely.

"Aha," said Lennon. "You can't tell now, can you?"

Lennon's efforts to bring attention to the war were a joke to some, but not to President Nixon. Lennon went on Nixon's list of enemies. The Immigration and Naturalization Service denied him a green card. The FBI built a file on him, followed him, eavesdropped on his phone conversations. They even sent out a memo to the Miami police urging them to try and arrest Lennon on drug possession charges, since the case for deporting him to England was "loose." But the FBI never frightened Lennon into silence. He started an ad campaign, paid for it out of his own pocket, and placed posters all over New York City that said, "War is Over! If You Want It." He even went on to write one of his best songs, a Christmas tune called "Happy Xmas (War Is Over)."

And a few years later, it *was* over.

When I was twelve, I once made the mistake of telling my mother that sixties music was stupid, that it was childish. I had been cranking up my vinyl copy of *Chicago X* and was feeling superior. Outraged, she sat me down in a chair and made me listen to Bob Dylan and Joan Baez tunes for an hour. A lot of songs about peace and love and workers' rights and something blowing in the wind. It all sounded a little bogus, and I didn't really get it. "You have to understand the time," she insisted. "The country was divided—ripped in two, really. Vietnam. The Kennedy assassination. Young people believed that music—just one voice and a guitar—could make sense of things, could make a difference. It could even change the world."

She told me a story I'd heard before, about how four years earlier she was in a parade with hundreds of other women. She carried a banner that said "Equal Pay for Equal Work." Mom and one of her friends supposedly held up bras and set them aflame with cigarette lighters.

"Are you listening?" she asked.

"I hope it was a spare."

"Hmm?"

"Your bra," I explained. "I hope you were wearing another one underneath your sweater and that the one you burned was a spare."

She placed her hand on the side of my face and turned me so I was looking at her. "The *point*," she said, "is while yes, maybe we were a little naïve, we made a difference, and the *music* made a difference. Joan Baez singing 'Joe Hill' focused us on making working conditions better. Dylan's song 'Blowin' in the Wind' focused us on ending a war."

"When did Dylan write 'Blowin' in the Wind'?" I asked.

Mom had to think for a minute. "Hmmm...1962."

"So he wrote it in '62, and you told me the war ended in 1974. Twelve years? That's not a very fast-working song."

"Don't be a smart-ass."

Mom really believed everything she said: One person, especially one person holding a guitar (or a flaming bra), could accomplish anything. He or she could change the world by sheer effort of will.

All of which, no doubt, explains the time my mother thought she could be a plumber.

"A plumber?" asks Dr. Artaud.

"Delusions of grandeur, in my mom's case," I add.

Dr. Artaud leans back in her chair, smiling as she scribbles something down on her pad. As she does, I glance at her wall clock and see I've been chattering for forty minutes. No session has ever passed this quickly, and I'm positive it's because I haven't closed my mouth since I walked in. So much talking on my part is highly unusual, though I can see that it pleases Dr. Artaud.

"Tell me about it," she says. "Your mother, the plumber." She taps the eraser of her pencil against the pad. She's been flipping through page after page this afternoon, filling up one sheet then moving on to the next like an inspired novelist.

"Well," I begin, "we didn't have any dishwashing powder..."

☆

Mom leans against the refrigerator. She nibbles on the nail of her right index finger, the only nail she ever chews, and stares down at the kitchen linoleum. Her eyes follow a trail of spots: a dark one the size of a quarter, where she spilled some coffee; a faint pink one in the vague shape of my hand, from when I slipped while holding a jelly sandwich; a yellow plop of old orange juice; some mud tracked in on my sneakers.

"This floor is filthy," Mom says. "I should clean it."

"Yes," I say, "it's filthy," and I nod solemnly.

I am nine years old.

"That having been said—"says my mother. She's talking to me but not *really* talking to me. She's just sort of thinking aloud in my direction. "It would better to wash the dishes first, don't you think? We can make lunch while the dishwasher is running, and *then* I'll clean the floor. That way we'll be done making messes until dinnertime, and the floor will stay cleaner longer, right?"

I can't fault the logic. Mom is a master at putting off the jobs she finds most unpleasant. She accomplishes this by finding other jobs, ones she deems easier or more enjoyable, that need doing first.

"Righto, Roundo," I say. This is one of my favorite expressions. I have no explanation for it, other than I like the echo of the *O* sounds and the way the *T* and the *D* click off the roof of my mouth.

Mom reaches under the sink and takes out a shiny green box of dishwasher soap, which she shakes. Something inside makes a dry scratchy sound, like my Frosted Flakes when only two or three flakes remain in the box. She taps her knuckle against the cardboard, and it thumps like a drum. "Hmm," she says.

Her eyes light on the plastic bottle that sits on the kitchen counter, filled with an amber-colored liquid.

"This'll probably work," she says.

The idea gets my unconditional support: "Righto, Roundo."

She opens the door to the dishwasher and pours maybe a tablespoon's worth of liquid dishwashing soap into the dispenser box. The box looks so big, and the little dollop of soap looks so…*insignificant.* Mom frowns and pours in just a bit more. Then, without a care, she closes the dishwasher and sets it running.

Smiling, she turns to me. "PB and J," she asks, "or Spaghetti-Os?"

The Ballad of John and Yoko

I opt for the second choice. We make lunch. We discuss Scooby-Doo. She does magic—pours a package of crystals into a pitcher of water, and the water turns to lemonade. I drag out a box of Girl Scout cookies and scarf one before the Spaghetti-Os are warm.

While she's looking for a clean bowl, I see bubbles oozing from the dishwasher. They're seeping through the rubberized seam and beginning a slow march across the floor.

"Mom," I say, "the dishwasher's making bubbles."

Momentarily stunned, we both watch the experiment we've unknowingly created. The bubbles multiply. Some as big as billiard balls begin to roll toward us; others, the size of peas, float in the air, landing on the table, the counter, the curtains, even my hand when I reach out to touch one.

"Shouldn't we turn the dishwasher off?" I ask.

Mom takes two steps toward the dishwasher, gets soggy slippers, and again starts chewing her single chewable nail. "It hasn't got an on/off switch," she shouts. I'm not sure why she's shouting. I can hear her. Our problem is not that the dishwasher is *noisy*. "You turn it on by latching the door," she says, "and you turn it off by *un*latching the door."

Or by waiting until the cycle is finished. Now I get it. She can't turn the dishwasher off, because unlatching the door would send an ocean of foamy water across the kitchen linoleum. She can't let the cycle finish because—well, we're already getting an idea what *that* looks like.

"Ah-*hah!*" Mom says. She slides—literally, over the wet floor—to a drawer by the fridge. She digs into it with one hand, which finally comes out gripping a pair of channel lock pliers. She holds them up as though they are some kind of tomahawk or club. She's going to battle. "I am Woman, hear me roar," she says dryly. She gets down on her knees in front of the sink, soaking her pants from the thigh down. It's only when she opens the cupboard below the sink that I see what she has in mind. In front of her are three water shutoff valves. One is for the hot, one is for the cold, and a third one, which sits off to the side, goes directly into the dishwasher.

Mom sticks her head under the sink, so that all I see are her calves, the heels of her shoes, and her butt waggling back and forth as she works. She's trying to hand-crank the last valve, shut off the flow of water to the dishwasher, and starve the bubbles to death.

"Take this as a lesson, Pamela," she says. "A woman can accomplish anything if she puts her mind to it. She doesn't need *help*. She doesn't need a *man*..."

"Last week you begged your boyfriend Syke to come over, and he had to bring about twelve different tools."

Mom stops clanging around. "Okay," she says, "remember this: I'm the mom. You're the kid. And that thing about the lawnmower was not my fault." Her head disappears inside the cabinet again, and I see her grip the valve with her hand. "As I was saying," she continues, "you have your mind. You have your strength..."

I guess her strength isn't quite enough, because the valve doesn't move. It's rusted tight. "Never fear," Mom says. She hefts the channel locks, adjusting them around the valve's handle. She grips them, grunting with the effort of turning it.

And then I hear a sound like a branch snapping, only more hollow and metallic.

Mom shrieks, and a fountain of water hits her in the chest and sends her tumbling backwards. It catches her in the face, drenches her hair, soaks her blouse. She fends it off with her hands, but it sprays around them and between her fingers. The water gushes out at high pressure and in the shape of a fan. Mom sputters, soggy hair in her face, and crawls into the spray. Eyes closed, she jams her arm under the sink and finds the other shutoffs. These have been used more recently, and so they turn by hand—though with obvious effort. Mom says *"Hhn!"* with every turn. The fan shape grows smaller, and smaller still, until it becomes a trickle, then stops entirely. Mom heaves back on her haunches and swipes her palm across her face. The water she wipes off hits the water on the floor with a slapping sound.

I roll around, squealing in the wetness, soaking my jeans and shirt. Until now Mom was having nearly *all* the fun.

"Are you okay?" I ask. I'm lying flat on my stomach on the wet floor, my elbows jammed downward and my face in my hands.

Mom's jeans, which had been a nice faded color when they were dry, are now navy blue. Little bubbles ooze from the pockets. She was wearing mascara, so now she looks like a lady with a questionable reputation or someone with two black eyes. "Fine," she says hoarsely. "Just fine." And she coughs.

Now, my mother is not stupid. She is not helpless, and she is not inclined to panic. I have never known her to live her life as though it were an episode of *I Love Lucy* or *Laverne & Shirley*. So I am a little surprised at the way the kitchen looks right now. My best explanation for what she has just done is that the sudden attack from the dishwasher caught her unawares, that she was so intent on protecting me, her precious child, from imminent drowning, that she failed to see the obvious. I figure there's no harm now in pointing it out. I get up, walk over to the dishwasher, and stare at the round knob you turn to start the wash cycle. When I twist it clockwise, it moves through a series of ratcheting sounds that end with a little *ding!*

None of this is my fault, so I'm not sure why Mom looks like she wants to kill me. A string of sopping, wavy hair dangles in front of her nose, dripping a steady stream of water that pitter-patters against the wet linoleum.

She grabs a mop, I reach for some old towels, and together we wipe down the floor. In twenty minutes the mess is cleaned up. We stand, arm in arm and damp to the skin, admiring our work.

"Floor looks clean," I say.

Mom hugs me against her and kisses my soggy head. "Yes, sweetie," she says, "the floor is clean."

Dr. Artaud, smiling at the story, jots a final note on her pad. "Well," she says, "today has been a bit of a breakthrough session, Star. I'm not sure what's different about this afternoon, but you've certainly been loquacious."

"Loquacious?"

"You have been talking quite a bit. It's a little out of character."

I nod.

I wonder what Dr. Artaud would think if she knew the part of the story I *hadn't* told her. The truth is, I left out the end. Mom wanted to prove to me that, though she had made a mistake with the dishwasher, her main point was correct. She could handle the problem; she could handle it herself. That afternoon she went to the hardware store and bought a little do-it-yourself plumbing book. She also bought a new valve, a good wrench, and a tube of pipe cement. She replaced the valve with no one's help—just me standing by holding the instructions open—and it hasn't leaked a drop since. She made me watch. She had to show me that she had been right all along.

And now, as I'm standing in the doorway to Dr. Artaud's office, and as her hand gently guides me out, I think of that thirty minutes I spent watching my mother fix the plumbing. And then I think of a guitar sitting in pieces in Teri Seegar's shop.

"Star?" says Dr. Artaud.

"Hmm?"

"Not that it isn't a welcome sight," she says, "but…why are you smiling?"

9

Ticket to Ride

Taking the bus to Seegar's Guitar Repair involves forty minutes worth of patience and a jumble of transfers. At the end of it all, the closest I get is a stop in front of a Denny's two blocks away. I take them at a run.

The bell zing-zings my presence. I find Teri standing at the counter with a customer. She's holding a guitar I'd recognize on any stage, in any photo. It's a Martin D-35; I can see the weird three-piece back, a dark triangle of rosewood set between two pieces of a slightly lighter shade. Teri turns it over, strums through some jazz chords I would love to learn, then hands the guitar to her customer. He's forty-something, balding, with the back of his hair pulled into a long ponytail. He blasts through a bluegrass lick, holding the guitar high up into his armpit to avoid scratching the wood on his giant belt buckle. The face of the guitar is dark brownish gold, the sound hole striped with lighter areas where his strumming has nicked it.

"Perfect," he says.

"Three twenty-five," says Teri.

I feel a rush of relief that surprises me. I had taken a liking to Teri, but only now do I realize just how tense I've been about leaving the guitar with her. I never asked myself, if I were to let her repair it, what sort of job would she do? I don't know her, don't know her reputation; my only measure of her skill is the fact that she owns this business. But I know the look of a Martin; I've drooled over enough of them in my many visits to music stores. When new, the tops are almost pure white. It's only after decades of playing they turn that beautiful gold color. Their sound grows louder and mellower. They become *more* expensive to purchase. If this man in the ponytail trusted her to work on such a precious instrument, I suppose I can suck up my own anxiety.

"Lotta money," the man says, writing a check.

"Only two kinds of vintage guitars," says Teri. "Those that need a neck reset—"

"—and those that need another," finishes the man. He tears out the check and hands it to her, smiling. He then sets the guitar in a beat-up case covered with old bumper stickers and carries it with both hands out the door.

"Hi, Teri," I say.

She curls her finger at me. "You come here," she says. "I have something to show you." She says this with a sly half smile and the same tone my mother would use when she was about to hand over my birthday present. I slip behind the counter and follow Teri through a doorway.

The hum of humidifiers is louder here. I see two, one in each corner. They're bigger than the one out front, made of metal, and they growl as they work. I smell sawdust, which I like, along with hints of metal and grease, which make me crinkle my nose. Several guitars in various stages of repair rest on stands or hang from rubber-coated hooks. Two worktables with carpeted surfaces sit in the middle of the concrete floor. Sheets of wood, some dark red-brown and some the color of ivory, lie flat across pallets. I follow Teri, weaving through a room filled with strange and wonderful machines. A few look moderately familiar—saws or planers of some kind—but others could be pieces from a crashed alien spaceship. One is in the vague shape of a guitar body, only it's metal. A weird conglomeration of clamps and bolts lines its edges.

"What is this?" I ask.

"It's a torture device," says Teri. "I use it to make a guitar tell me everything I want to know—or else." She smiles, waiting for me to react to the joke. I don't. The truth is, I'm nervous about the repair and especially about the money. Teri sighs. "It's a guitar form, Star. A wood-bender. Haven't you ever wondered how they get the sides of a guitar to bend the way they do?"

I shrug. "Not really."

"Hmph," says Teri. "Pity. Well, that's how. Let me show you your guitar."

I see my mother's Gibson now, resting flat on a cloth-covered table. We walk over, and Teri rubs her hand along the top of it. "Do this," she says.

I trail my fingers from the lower bout to the sound hole, and then to the fingerboard. It takes a second touch before I feel what she wants me to feel. *"Hey."* I bend at the knees so that I'm level with the soundboard, and my eye confirms what my fingers told me: The dip in the top is gone. If anything, it now has a slight arch to it.

"Good," says Teri. "You see it."

I notice more changes when I pick the guitar up. The neck, though still separated from the body, fits into its opening like a well-made puzzle piece. No more jiggling. And yes, a four-inch crack still follows the seam where the top meets the side, but the edges of the crack have joined; it's no longer a jagged mouth. I run my fingers across the strings. They jangle at a higher pitch, suggesting they're tauter than they were.

"What did you do?" I ask. In my mind, I'm wondering, *and what are you going to charge me?*

"Nothing, really," she says. "I took your guitar, plus three little plastic guitar humidifiers, and stuck them all in a trash bag for four days. For the last three days it's been drying out. The wood is back to its proper moisture content. Now, if you want, we can go to work on it."

I look again at the damage, the neck that needs resetting, the crack that needs repair, the split and broken ribs—all salvageable for only five hundred dollars.

I rub my hand across the fingerboard. "Is it worth fixing?" I whisper.

"Sweetie," she says, "it's a vintage Gibson."

And of course, that says it all. It's a vintage Gibson. It's a fine guitar made finer by the very fact that it's lived this long. Teri and I both understand that I can't say no to fixing it—and not just because it's a fine guitar, but because it once belonged to my mother. It could be a Sears special. It could be plywood. It could be *plastic;* I'd still pay a fortune to fix it.

If I had a fortune.

I close my eyes and draw in a deep breath. I think of my arms around this guitar, the strings biting ridges into my fingertips. I think of its chunky, fat sound, the way it rang out in the midrange when my mother played, even when she played badly. I know, better than I've ever known anything, that I am supposed to have this guitar. I can see my mother—leather work gloves on her hands, adjusting her new wrench to fit around her new sink valve, plumbing book splayed open on the floor next to her—and I get the message. If I *need* to do something, I can do it. The task might take strength, patience, effort, or brains—or any combination of those qualities—but I can do it. If I am meant to have this guitar, I only have to wait until I find the gifts I need—the right idea, the right words, the right timing. When the moment comes, something will fall into place.

"Okay, here's my offer," I say.

The words surprise me, because I really didn't think before I spoke. *What* offer? Teri leans against a worktable and folds her arms, already defending herself against whatever I might throw at her.

"I'll pay for the materials," I say, "and...and I'll go to work for you. I'll sweep floors, wipe windows, take the trash out, clean the bathroom." I point to the worktable, to the loose tools scattered on it. "I'll put away your tools when you're finished with them—or do anything you need me to do. I'm not asking you to pay me. All you have to do is show me a little about guitar repair. I'll even, I don't know, do some of the repair work myself, as long as it's something I can't screw up too badly."

Teri is shaking her head even before I finish. Her arms fold in front of her like castle doors swinging shut. Her muscles tense. I get it: It's not that she's never considered having an apprentice. She *has* considered the idea—and pointedly rejected it, long before she met me. "Star, guitar repair isn't like fixing a flat tire," she says. "It's a *craft*. It's something you do out of love, and it takes years to learn." She gestures toward the torture device. "A minute ago you weren't even interested in the guitar form."

"I adore guitar forms," I say quickly. "I am brimming with fascination for guitar forms. I love the way they, you know, bend wood and all." I make my eyes as wide and pleading as I can. I think of animals in Disney cartoons. I'm Thumper. Who could turn down this face?

Teri laughs. Her eyes dart to a framed photograph that hangs on the wall over her worktable. They look away, then are drawn back. I look too. It's a photo of Teri, years younger, her arms around a guitar. Another woman sits next to her, hugging Teri's neck. The woman is a little heavier than Teri, but she has the same frizzy red hair and freckles, the same sharp little nose, the same wide-mouthed, totally unafraid smile. Teri is frozen, staring at the picture.

"That's your mother, isn't it," I say.

"Yes," says Teri. She wipes her hands on a cloth then reaches for a tiny plastic crank. As I watch, she takes my mother's guitar and places the crank, a string winder, over one of the tuning machines. The E string buzzes and twangs as she winds it down and slips it off the guitar. "I'll expect you Monday through Friday from four to six," she says, "and from ten to three on Saturday."

Panic flashes. I see tutoring. I see homework. I see Dr. Artaud twisting her pencil into her chin, disapproving.

"I can't do Thursdays," I say. "I'm..." I'm what? A cheerleader? A Math Club officer? No, it's a bad moment to lie. "Um...I'm in therapy."

Teri gives a little nod and tosses the crank to me. "Fine. No Thursdays. Now how about you crank off the rest of these strings?"

"Yes, ma'am," I say.

"Oh, honey, we are gonna do *sooo* much better if you never call me 'ma'am' again."

☆

I hate escalators. The handrail moves just a little faster than the steps, so I feel my arm straighten out more and more with each passing moment. I have to keep drawing it back. Normally I wouldn't complain. I'd pound up the moving steps, my hand just nipping at the rail every few inches for balance, and be on my way. Today, though, an elderly couple stands in front of me, side by side, and I don't have the heart or the energy to squeeze past. I stand behind them thinking about the money I just withdrew from my pitiful bank account.

Pepperland

I'm in May Company, moving between the second floor Ladies' Department and third floor Bedding and Furnishings. The metal stairs fold into themselves, and I almost stumble as the ground levels beneath me. Just ahead are the Credit Department and the Ticketron outlet. A girl with blue hair stands behind the counter. "May I help you?"

"Um, yes—I'd like a ticket to the Elton John concert at the Pavilion."

"One?"

"Yes, I'm not very popular."

The sales girl blushes.

I can't spring for two tickets. Dooley would go with me, of course, but he can't really afford to buy his own. Besides, considering what I'm planning to do the night of the show, it may be better that I go by myself. If a jail cell lies somewhere in my future, it might as well be single occupancy.

I could run all the way home. I could do back flips down the sidewalk and up the steps to my front door. I could sing, loudly, in front of a crowd at the mall, for no reason other than I feel like singing. I could kiss Dooley on the mouth. I could kiss Syke on the cheek. If not for the impression it might create, I could lay a big lipstick smack on Teri Seegar. It's a good thing a stranger isn't walking past me right now, all things considered. I'm flying. Oh yeah, a hint of sadness creeps around the edge of this picture, but it's only a tiny, distant voice screaming that the joy I'm feeling won't last, and that I won't know how to make it return. I ignore it. My mother died three months ago, and today is the first day the world has felt a little bit right again.

Ticket to Ride

The bus lurches underneath me. My head's been every-where except here, where I'm sitting. Instead of watching traf-fic, I've been imagining my arms around my mother's guitar. A voice—*mine? Is my voice that pretty?*—sings a hymn to her. The tune is vague, and I can't make out the words, but the song is beautiful. It's slow and lilting, like the Irish cadence in my mother's speech.

I glance out the window. Is it possible I've reached my stop already? I tug the overhead cable and hop from my seat as the doors open. I grin stupidly at the driver as I leave. I don't know why. The sun is setting, the sky is gray-blue, and it just feels like a lovely evening for grinning stupidly.

Five minutes later I'm home. The moment I open the front door I can tell Syke's puttering in the kitchen. I can hear some-thing sizzling on the stove. The house smells like onion and garlic. Behind the heavy spices is a whiff of something sweet—warm apples, and maybe cinnamon. He's doing dessert, too. His leather jacket lies over the back of the couch. He's feeling casual. Van Morrison on the stereo means he's had a good day. I toss my backpack onto the living room chair, even though I know that half an hour from now Syke will demand that I move it so he can watch television.

"I'm home!"

"Door slam already told me," he calls back.

"Sorry!"

I rush to my bedroom and grab my Tele from its stand. I have a little while before dinner, and I want to feel it hanging from my shoulders, my hand along its neck, strings crying under my fingertips. I have a neon green cable, which I plug into my little Pignose amp, and I play a single power chord. It feels good, but not a perfect match to my excitement, so I click on the distortion and hit it again. I jump into the air as I strike the strings, my pitiful attempt at rock stardom. It's the last beat of a song, and the bass and drums crash together as my final chord rings out. The audience goes wild. I play "Over the Hills and Far Away" by Led Zeppelin. I play "Aqualung" by Jethro Tull. I play "Smoke on the Water," which will get you thrown out of most guitar shops, the employees are so sick of hearing kids fumble it.

The phone rings twice. I let Syke answer.

In terms of helping me heal my mind and heart, Dr. Artaud is good, but music is better. She's right when she says that I hide behind music. I sometimes let sound get physical, so that it rings in my ears and vibrates in my chest and drowns out the unhappy voices in my head. Other times, like right now, music helps me respond to my better voices, the ones that give me a squeeze to the shoulders and a gentle push ahead.

Music is an act of creation. A musician gives life to a song, even if he or she didn't write it. I would say that learning to play someone else's song is different from writing one yourself, a different kind of commitment. Syke would say it's like raising an adopted child.

From the other room, his voice rises in volume, and it has an edge to it that worries me. I set the guitar on its stand and move down the hallway toward the kitchen.

"We don't work that way," says Syke. His voice rumbles. "Our bid is in. We either get the job or we don't." Syke is a contractor, and he still does a lot of hands-on construction work. Right now he's wearing a sweatshirt with the sleeves cut off at the shoulder, revealing his huge arms and the U.S. Marines tattoo on his left shoulder. It's safe to figure that whoever he's talking to would be taking a different attitude if the two stood face-to-face.

I'm close enough to hear buzzing from the phone's earpiece. The cord is in a tangle over Syke's shoulder, and he twists it with his free hand as he paces between the table and the stove. He looks like he's two sentences away from ripping the cord from the wall. "Mike, what am I saying here that's so hard to understand?" Then he snarls, "Look, I'm through talking about this. *Fix* it. Whatever you gotta do, fix it." I jerk back from his tone. In all the time I've known him, Syke has only raised his voice to me once or twice—and never like this. I'm looking at a stranger.

"What's going on?" I mouth.

He slams down the phone, sees me, and catches himself. He doesn't answer my question; he just runs a hand across his bald head as though he's ruffling his hair. Now he turns toward the fridge. He opens it, stares dully into its yellow light, then closes it as if he'd just remembered he didn't need anything from there after all. A stutter-step toward the table. Now to the faucet. He turns his back to me, and a moment later I hear a loud metallic clatter as he tosses a pan into the sink. I smell something bitter. While he's been on the phone, he's ignored the vegetables, and they've burned.

"Syke?"

He calms somewhat and begins putting food on the table. The blackened veggies are still in the sink, but he's scooping out the ones that are moderately edible and slopping them into a Tupperware bowl. A serving plate in the middle of the table already bears three pork chops—one for me and two for him. He even starts setting out plates and dinnerware, which is my job. One plate bangs on the tabletop, rattling as it comes to rest.

"Here," I say, "I'll do that."

He sits and waits for me. I fill plates and grab napkins for both of us, pour soft drinks from a two-liter bottle. Now I'm sitting next to him, the food is ready to eat, and all I can do is hold my fork in my fist. Syke is doing the same, and I have this idiotic thought that we look like the farmer couple in that painting *American Gothic*—sad, tired, and maybe a little confused about how we got where we are. I don't know what happened just now on the phone. I just know that Mike, the guy on the other end of the line, is Syke's business partner. They've known each other longer than I've been on this planet. They're friends. They never argue over anything more serious than Tastes Great/Less Filling.

"So what happened?" I ask.

"Nothing," says Syke. "Nothing, really. Some lumber came in late. The job we were supposed to start today will have to wait until tomorrow."

"That's it? A one-day delay? That's what caused the explosion?"

In Syke's line of work, simple delays happen all the time. So now I get it: Syke's distress, his confusion, is not about the delay—it's about the fight itself. I hear Dr. Artaud's voice coming back to me: *And how is your arm feeling?* I see all of my own flashes of anger and stupidity—the punch to the fridge, the tornado in my bedroom, the Sloppy Joe meltdown. I never told Syke about the session when Dr. Artaud asked, "Who are you mad at, Star?" And I definitely never told him the name I whispered. I'm just holding onto it, letting it simmer in my brain. Now I'm looking at Syke's blank face and wondering if it isn't time to talk about it.

"You don't usually get this mad," I say. "You know, about little stuff."

He jabs his fork into a corner of his pork chop and saws at it with his knife.

"Is something else going on?"

The meat goes into his mouth. He chews, swallows, jabs at his meal again.

"Syke?"

"It's nothing. All right?"

"Because maybe we should—"

"It's just business. It happens."

"Syke, what I'm saying is—"

"I don't want to discuss it!"

"But maybe if we—"

His hand comes down on the tabletop—*bang!* Plates jump. Dinnerware clatters. My insides make the same kind of sound. Pepsi sloshes over the rim of my glass and into my salad. I'm too scared to look at Syke directly, so I become strangely fascinated by the way the brown drink makes little streams and gullies through and around the lettuce in my bowl. Moments later, when I finally do look up, Syke is staring down at his hand as though he didn't expect it to be there, as though it's some weird object fallen out of a passing airplane. He draws it back. The moment limps past us.

"Are you okay?"

He nods. The hand disappears under the table.

"We never talk about her, Syke," I say. "Why is that?"

He sags a little in the chair. He doesn't say anything, but his lower jaw begins to quiver. Then he runs his hand along his mouth and the shaking stops. "I'm not very hungry," he says.

"Me neither."

We have dessert instead. We eat apple pie mounded over with ice cream. We eat it in front of the television set, and we turn up the volume and sit too close to the screen for our own good. We laugh too loudly, and we throw wadded napkins at the characters we don't like. Sure, Syke and I watch out for each other, but tonight we're rebels, and we're in it together.

10

I'm Looking Through You

I see Dooley moving toward me from the far end of the corridor. Around him, school seems normal. Kids slam locker doors. Mr. Kalidones, the chemistry teacher, leans against the wall outside his room, sipping coffee. A boy and a girl glance around, see no one is paying attention, then steal a kiss. Dooley becomes the center of this picture. Like a question on an IQ test, he is the Item That Doesn't Belong. He strides, head down, weight leaning forward, eyes on the floor. Invisible waves come off him that other students miraculously sense. They step aside or turn their bodies to allow him to pass. Dooley doesn't acknowledge them. He glowers. His eyes are ringed with pink skin.

"Dooley?"

"A-holes," he whispers. "Effing a-holes."

Dooley doesn't actually curse. Four-letter words embarrass him. They sometimes pop out, but he always stutters afterward—as though he's so caught up by the fact that he's said something naughty that he's lost track of the conversation. When he's really angry, he censors himself. He makes his own curse words by using the initials of the real thing. It's "effing" this and "effing" that.

"What happened?"

I'm Looking Through You

He looks over his shoulder at the crowded hallway, then angles his body so that his back is between us and anyone who might pass by. He's holding his art pad and his history book in one hand. "A-holes," he says again, and I see the pink around his eyes has darkened to red. Tears aren't running down his cheeks or anything, but his eyes are unnaturally shiny.

He turns over his history book.

My hand covers my mouth. I close my eyes and shake my head. How *stupid* can some people be? Our books have thick cardboard bindings, and it's a well-known fact that if you rub the cover hard enough with an eraser, the color image wears off, revealing the white cardboard underneath. You can make designs this way, or pictures. You can even spell out words. Some jerk—a definite a-hole—has decided to do just that with Dooley's book. Six-inch-tall shredded-white letters spell out the word "Fag." "Dooley...my god. How did this happen?"

"I was, um...I was in gym class," he says. He gulps in air between phrases. "I left my books on a bench in the locker room. Just for a few minutes—while I showered."

I nod.

"And someone did *this*. They did *this* to me."

He faces the wall and leans forward against it, banging his head twice, hard, on the brick.

"Dooley, stop that. Stop hurting yourself."

He just picks up the conversation, pretending the head-banging didn't happen. "They turned the book upside-down, so I wouldn't notice right away. They wanted me to go to my next class and flip it over in front of everybody, let the teacher—*everybody*—see it." He leans closer, and his voice kind of hisses in my ear. "It was Farris. It had to be."

"Farris is still in alternative school," I remind him. Alternative school students report to a separate building, which sits several hundred yards from the main school. They're not allowed to mix with the regular students—not during lunch, not even during class changes.

"Then one of his friends," Dooley adds.

"How could someone mess with your stuff without your seeing him?"

I know as soon as I ask that it's a stupid question. The gym classes are completely unmanageable—two coaches, sixty or seventy kids, everyone tossed onto the field or the black-topped basketball courts. Give them a dozen or so basketballs, a few soccer balls, and count the kids who dress out. End of the gym lesson.

"My mother's going to kill me," Dooley says.

And of course, he's right. Teachers check textbooks out to their students by name. We're responsible for taking care of them. If Dooley can't prove who vandalized his book, he'll not only have to live with the word rubbed into it, he'll have to pay for a replacement copy at the end of the semester. Double slap in the face.

The bell rings. I take Dooley by the elbow and drag him down the hall. "Come on," I say. "Let's not be late to class. We've got enough problems."

He takes a few steps with me, but then he resists, forcing me to turn and face him. "Star," he says, "why are they *doing* this? Do they really think—?"

"They don't think anything," I tell him. "You're smart, and they're not. You can paint, and they can't. It's nothing more than jealousy. You're different, okay? You're better than they are, and they can't stand it."

As I'm talking, an idea comes to me. I look around the hall and see that, while most students have dashed off to class, a couple of dozen stragglers still remain. They're talking, laughing, and only moderately interested in getting to class on time.

"Hey, everybody!" I shout. The hall is empty enough that my voice reverberates. Every head turns in my direction.

And I grab Dooley and kiss him flush on the lips for a full five seconds. I even hold him there with both hands just to make sure the message gets out that I'm enjoying it.

"Hey! Hey!" says Mr. Kalidones. Coffee blurps over the rim of his mug and wets the cuff of his shirt. "Stop that, you two! You know the rules."

I break away, smile and wave at the crowd, then take a very dazed Dooley by the hand and lead him off to class.

"What was that for?" he asks.

I just grin. "Let that confuse the hell out of them."

☆

Dooley doesn't meet me at the oak tree after school. He usually does—just to say a quick see ya before my bus arrives, or to ask if he can come over and play some music—but today he isn't there. I figure I have a few extra minutes, so I check the locker area and the parking lot. No sign of him. No luck in the library either, where they're having math tutoring. *Oops*, I think. I'm supposed to be brushing up on my polynomial-whatchamahoojies. I duck out quickly, before the algebra II teacher, Mr. Wingate, spots me and says, "Ms. Cochran, what a rare honor. Here's a chair with your name on it, I believe."

In the hallway I stop to catch my breath, and my mind sees what I've been missing. I know where Dooley is.

I head down a corridor lined with glass display cases and plastic poster frames. In the poster frames are pencil studies—student drawings of spheres and cubes and cylinders, all shaded to give the impression they are three-dimensional. Looking at them is a little too much like geometry homework, so I move past them quickly. The showcases, on the other hand, contain plaster of paris masks painted in bright colors. Some are clownlike. Others are elegant, like something a Renaissance-era lady might have worn to a ball. A few, with their sharp teeth and red mouths, seem primitive and frightening. My favorite is the last of the bunch. It has startled eyes, a blue tear on one cheek, and a single eyebrow that curls around the eye and then down along the cheekbone, transforming into a question mark.

Below it is a cardboard tag bearing the name of the artist: Sean O'Doul.

I can hear the voice of Mrs. Thomasson, the advanced art teacher, and I follow it into her room. She's chatting with a student. In the corner, working silently in front of an easel, is Dooley. He sees me at the door, hurriedly puts down his paintbrush, then covers the easel with a cloth.

"Hey," I say.

"Hey."

I study his face. I'm looking for clues as to how he's feeling, some whiff of "I'm okay" before I leave for the afternoon. Usually Dooley is a sheet of glass, but I'm not seeing anything right now.

"Just checking up on you," I say. "Are you all right?"

"I'm still mad about the book."

I nod. "I don't blame you."

An old wad of bubble gum, left over from the Jurassic period, is stuck on the floor in front of him. Dooley kicks at it with the toe of his shoe, but it's petrified, solid rock. I watch him for a few moments, waiting for him to lose patience with it. He finally stops, but he still won't look at me.

"I want to ask you something," he says.

"Okay."

"Are you...I mean, do you...um...about what those people say about me..."

I'm Looking Through You

"No," I say. "I mean, it's not the most articulate question you've ever asked, but I think I know where you're going, and the answer is no."

I watch his face, but still see nothing from him. He's the mask before anyone's painted a face on it. I feel the need to find some extra words, anything to get a response from him.

"It would be okay if you were. We'd still be friends, but…"

Now something happens: a flicker of panic crosses Dooley's eyes, then it's gone. I've said the wrong thing, so I shift into reverse. "I mean, *no.* No, I don't think that. C'mon, Dooley, I'm the girl who liplocked you this morning."

He laughs, which gives me a second to gather my wits. I use the time to change the subject. "So," I say, "what are you painting?"

"Nothing…it's nothing…"

"C'mon, show me…"

I start to tug at the cloth, but he presses down on it with his hands. "I don't want you to see it yet."

"Please?" I fake a wide grin and add fourteen syllables to the word. "Pleeeeeeaase?" As I'm whining, I continue tugging gently, giving him every chance to stop me if he truly doesn't want me to see the painting. He doesn't bother.

"Ooohh…" I draw in a sudden breath when I see it. Before me is a portrait of a young woman. She is strikingly beautiful, her face nearly white and her cheekbones shaded in an icy pale blue. Her eyes are large and pretty, but dark and a little wounded-looking. She's not really smiling. Behind her is a background of burgundy and violet. Within this background, and over the girl's face, are crossing lines, like the squares on a sheet of graph paper. It's as if little parts of her have been painted on hundreds of tiles, and the tiles have assembled themselves to make this image. Except in the upper left-hand corner, the pattern breaks down. The tiles are scattered, the

lines no longer forming perfect angles. The pieces seem to be falling, cascading into place. The girl is in the process of becoming a complete picture.

"It's beautiful," I whisper.

And then I understand. I see it.

The girl with the wounded eyes, the girl who doesn't quite smile, the girl made of a thousand pieces that are falling, at last, into their proper places…

She's me.

I don't know how to behave around Teri Seegar. She wears glasses and mens' shirts with the sleeves rolled and the tails untucked. She has narrow lips that make her look a little hard inside and unhappy, and she moves too fast. When she's bending over a guitar, as she is right now, she has the care and precision of a figure skater. Her fingers glide across the wood; her eyes meander down a neck, checking for straight lines. Then the phone rings, or a customer enters, and she's off again. She makes me nervous. I guess she's just a little too *new* to me, and like my mother's guitar, I'm still adjusting to the air in here.

She's removing a bolt-on neck from an old Stratocaster copy. "Where's my five-eighths wrench?" she asks. Her speech has a *rat-tat-tat* rhythm to it, like a snare drum. "I had it right here, now what did I do with it?" She's not really talking to me. She's talking to herself. She hasn't adjusted to my presence any more than I have to hers.

I pause in my sweeping and nod toward the panel of pegboard over her worktable. Tools hang there from little hooks. She'll find her five-eighths right where it belongs, between the three-eighths and the seven-eighths. I know, because I put it there twenty minutes ago. I say none of this, of course.

"Ah," she says, "here it is. Hmm...a place for everything, and everything in its place, huh, Star? This *will* take some getting used to."

She's nice, though. During a lull she let me play her guitar with the vine inlay, and she showed me those jazz chords I admired. My fingers don't like them yet. She also sent me across the street for some sandwiches, and she paid for mine even though it wasn't part of our deal.

"Okay, Star," she says, "put the broom up. It's time for lesson number one."

She gently lifts my mother's guitar from its case and sets it on the worktable, fitting a padded block under the neck. Without the strings, it looks even sadder and emptier than I remember, like a body without a soul. Together Teri and I huddle over it, and once again she shines a flashlight into the sound hole. "Before we do anything about the neck," she says, "we have to make sure the body, especially the top, is structurally sound. That means we start with these broken braces. See that tube of glue over there? Grab it for me."

As I hand her the tube, I glance at the label. "Titebond? Is this good stuff?"

She smiles. "Nah, it's just really cheap."

"*What?*"

"I'm kidding. Hand me that little bin over there."

On her workbench is a plastic bin containing what looks like dozens of tiny blocks of wood. Each one, I see, has a deep V shape cut into it. Some of the Vs are wide, some narrow. When I hand the bin to Teri, she reaches in for one block, holding it to the light.

"What are those?" I ask.

"Fittings for my clamps. When you fix guitars for a living, finding the right tool can be a pain. Sometimes you just have to make your own."

She shows me that to reglue the braces in my mother's guitar, she has to hold them together with a metal clamp while the glue dries. Teri's little hand-carved blocks rest against the odd angle of the brace on one side and the flat surface of the clamp on the other. A perfect fitting.

Now she's reaching for a plastic syringe. Connected to the tip of the syringe is a long, transparent tube.

"Another homemade tool?" I ask.

"The syringe came with some liquid medicine the vet gave me for my dog," Teri admits. "The flexible tubing came from a toy radio-controlled car."

She reveals more tricks—like the mirror she's cut into three pieces and then put back together with duct tape. Now the mirror folds like a wallet. She slips it through the sound hole of the guitar, and once it's in, she opens it to its full size. A string of tiny white Christmas tree lights follows. When she plugs them in, the inside of the guitar blazes with light.

"That's so smart!"

Now she draws up a small amount of Titebond into the syringe. "Here comes the tricky part," she says. "Come on over and take a look." She leans over and, peering into the sound hole, begins injecting a thin line of glue where one of the braces has split. "You don't need a lot," she says. "A little will hold the crack. There...and there..." She makes several deft motions with the syringe, then reaches into the sound hole with her free hand, holding the glued brace together. "Hand me that clamp," she says, pointing. "No, the long, narrow one. That's it." Teri fits it on, turns a screw at one end, and the clamp tightens. It will hold the x-brace in position until the Titebond hardens.

"Is that it?" I ask.

"Nope," she says. "Now we do the crack in the top." The expression on Teri Seegar's face reminds me of the witch in "Hansel and Gretel," who, in a picture book I read as a child, smiles wickedly as she offers the children a plate of cookies. Like the witch, Teri does the incredible, the unthinkable, and does it for the sheer enjoyment of terrifying me.

She hands me the syringe filled with glue. "Your turn," she says.

"Really? Now? I'm feeling faint. Would you call 911, please?"

"Star..."

"But this is on the *outside*," I tell her. "The brace was *inside*. Who cares if there's a glue ball there? No one will see it. But here—"

"If it happens, we'll fix it."

I'm doomed. The woman is impossible. The crack—right where that beautiful spruce top meets the mahogany body—is waiting. Under protest, I squirt a thin line of glue along it with a shaky hand, then close my eyes as Teri presses the crack together. "Spool clamp," she says. "It looks like a post with a big knob at either end."

I hand her a spool clamp, and she tightens it down over the crack. By the time she's finished, she's used three, which now force down an even pressure along the crack's entire length. "Look, Star," she says, wiping away a glue ball. "No glue balls. You did it perfectly."

I curtsy. "Thank you. I am going to kill you now."

"Was it that bad?"

"Terrifying. What are you going to have me do next, eye surgery?"

Teri lets out a short bark of a laugh, an explosion of air from her gut.

We both glance at the wall clock. It's straight-up six, time to go home. I surprise myself: The thought of leaving now truly disappoints me. I've enjoyed being around all the guitars, the customers with their finicky requests, the smells of wood, and especially Teri. We're not accustomed to each other yet, but I guess now that I've threatened to kill her we at least have room to grow.

I turn to gather my things. On a nearby wall I see a framed picture, one I hadn't noticed earlier. I get close enough to see that it contains a publicity shot of Teri alongside a page cut from *Billboard* magazine. It's the Top Forty listing for the week of February 19, 1972. Number twelve, highlighted in red, is a song called "Makin' It or Breakin' It," by Teri Seegar. I blink several times before the name registers.

"Wait...you had a top forty record?"

"Uh-huh," she says. "Remember when Carly Simon came out with 'Anticipation'?"

"Yeah, I was around eight."

"Okay, now remember when Carole King came out with 'Sweet Seasons'?"

"Umm...sort of."

"Well, my song held that spot on the chart for about fifteen minutes, between those two."

"You say it like it's nothing." I touch my hand to the glass, underline her name with my fingernail. "You were *here*. You charted. People heard you on the radio. That's really something."

She stands close to me, staring at the chart. Her thin-lipped smile makes her look sad. "Yeah, hon, it was that, all right. It wasn't all I thought it would be, the way I imagined it in my head while I was working for it, but it was something."

11

This Boy

Once again I can't find Dooley at school. At first I think he might be having one of his emotional rants, the kind that makes him hole up in one the boys' room stalls. He told me once that, when he's really bothered by something, he leaves class and heads to the restroom. He closes the door to the stall, puts down the seat to make a chair, and just sits there with his head bent down and his hands over his eyes to make everything black. I sort of understand. I know what it's like to want to make some quiet space around myself, so Dooley's restroom meditations never seemed too terribly strange.

During lunch I try the library and computer lab, the oak tree and the art room. I can't find him. If he's in the middle of one of his restroom trances, I'll just have to wait.

In fifth period Mr. Bequeworth passes out the vocabulary lesson, and I ask to see the daily announcements. On the back of the sheet is a list of the day's excused absences, so teachers can see if a student is home sick or just cutting an afternoon class. He hands me the list, but his thick forefinger taps the vocab sheet on my desk as a warning: *Stay focused! You, Star Cochran—after some bad grades, one lame essay, and two days in ISS—have little room for messing up!* Mr. Bequeworth is tall and round-faced, and he has a wispy-blond elf beard. Still, he manages to pack a good deal of threat into a tiny gesture.

I wait until he's fiddling with the overhead projector before I steal a glance at the sheet. In the second column, twelve names down among the list of juniors, I find Dooley's name. He's home. Worse, he's alone, and he's probably sick.

I'm a mass of guilt for the next two hours. In my mind I see Dooley on his deathbed. He's thin and hollow-cheeked; his skin shines with perspiration. I dwell on this thought, and my guilt takes the image further. I begin to see him with tubes coming out of his nose; I hear the steady *ping* of a heart monitor next to him. I drive the image from my mind. I don't want to feel as though I am wishing pain on Dooley—and besides, this last picture is a little too close to memories of my mom.

During sixth period I begin to wonder why I'm torturing myself so. I'm staring at a mind-numbing slide show on the three branches of government when I finally work out the answer: I'm punishing myself because only a few days ago I would have jumped on a different bus when school was over. I would have rung the driver two blocks from Dooley's apartment, and I would have sprinted up the stairs to his door. He would have greeted me in pajamas, robe, and mussed hair, and the two of us would have sat at far ends of the couch, making fun of the afternoon soap operas or the 1950s Western on channel five. I'm punishing myself because this day will be different. I won't be at Dooley's at all this afternoon. I'll be looking after myself instead. I'll be at Teri's shop, and I'll be cleaning something or putting something away or gluing something that needs gluing, and thoughts of Dooley, I'm afraid, will not even cross my mind. That's why I feel guilty. Some days it seems that all of life is a battle over what gets your attention—your own needs, or someone else's. Already I can feel the shift: Instead of Dooley with a nose full of sterile plastic, I see a guitar, so polished it throws light into your eyes when you look at it. I feel the strings, tight and solid beneath my fingers. I hear myself singing.

I feel awful about it—terrible, really—but today I win. I come first.

☆

"Now we deal with the neck," says Teri.

She holds a notched steel tool against the fingerboard of my guitar, the notches matching the position of the fret wires. I can see daylight in places where the tool doesn't touch the wood.

"Is it supposed to look like that?" I ask.

Teri tugs the loose neck a bit, wrestling with it. I hear wood squeak against wood. "It should lie flush to the board," she says. "And just touch the bridge at the other end."

The next hour or so involves steaming the guitar until the old glue weakens completely and the neck falls off. Later, when the wood has dried out, Teri measures, shaves off tiny bits of wood here, shims the neck there, and measures again. After twenty minutes of working, eyeballing, working, she reaches for the tool again to make a final adjustment.

Then she jerks her head in the direction of the Titebond. "Time for more glue."

"I'll get it."

We're learning not to step on each other in the work area. I can sense now what tool she needs, or how she might move from one end of the work table to the other, even when she might suddenly stick her butt out, which she does every time she bends down to eye a guitar's neck. It's a dance. I turn sideways as I pass her, somehow knowing she's going to reach for a peg winder or a clamp.

The neck reset is the most delicate job we've done. I bring the glue then stand off at a distance, watching. Teri spreads it thinly within the neck joint, and then she fits the neck back into place, eyeing, measuring, eyeing again. She works the two pieces until they no longer look like two at all, as though the neck and body came from a single chunk of tree.

"Clamp," she says, and I'm already handing it to her.

The thought of Dooley hits me again. He's home sick with no one to care for him. I also remember the kiss I laid on him in the hallway at school, and I find myself wondering if he's my boyfriend. Is he? Should he be? A part of me warms to the idea. It would be nice to have someone to hold and to kiss. On the other hand, he is Dooley, with all the moodiness and hypersensitivity that comes with him.

"Teri, are you married?" I ask.

"Been, was, and done with it," she says.

"You're divorced?"

"By default. My husband was a trucker. One day he went out trucking and never came back. Had to hire a private investigator to find out that he was shacking up with a waitress in Arizona." She points to a guitar hanging from a hook. "Would you crank the strings off that Washburn for me?"

I reach for the peg winder. The Washburn is heavy, and I like the feel of it. "So you two worked out a settlement?"

"Not much to work out," she says. "Just cut each other loose, is all."

I think of my bio-dad. I think of Dooley scaring me with his vampire kiss. "Are all guys like that?"

"Like what?"

"Assholes."

She laughs. "Don't know *all* of them."

The D string on the Washburn sings as I unwind it, pitching

downward until it's a metallic buzz against the wood. "The ones you've known?"

Teri pauses and thinks. "Yup," she finally says. "Every one." She's deliberately poking at me. She can hardly keep a straight face.

"Oh, come *on*. I'm sixteen. You're going to turn me into an angry, cynical, man-hater before I'm twenty. I need a little sunlight between the clouds here."

"Allen wrench," she says.

"*Teri!*"

I hand her the wrench, and she slips it into the sound hole of the Washburn, does a minor tweaking to the truss rod. "Relationships aren't pretty, hon," she says. "They can really tear you up. But I do have some sunlight for you."

"What's that?"

She holds up the guitar, staring down its neck and pointing it at me like a rifle. "They make for some great songs," she says. "They make for some *damn* great songs."

You can track John Lennon's relationships, I think, by looking at the music. Who was the girl he wanted so much it made him sorry? Who was the girl who gave him no reply? Who was the girl who wore red—and made him blue? Who was his baby in black? Who made him feel all right after a hard day's night? Who taught him that he had to hide his love away, and why should he have known better? Who bought a ticket to ride?

The later songs are easy—they're Yoko, all Yoko. But what about the earlier songs, the ones he wrote before he met the love of his life? Is there an individual connected to every one of them, dozens of women inspiring dozens of hits? Or did one woman—maybe his first wife, Cynthia—color the early part of his life, giving him so many different experiences that she served as the inspiration for all the songs? Sometimes, as I listen to Mom's old records, I make a game of attaching faces to the words. Some faces, in my imaginings, are women from Lennon's own life. Some are mysterious—dark and veiled women seen from a distance. Some are angry, yelling out their humiliation at being thrown before an audience on radio or record. When I'm most lost, and when the song is particularly beautiful, the women in my fantasies have my mother's face.

Maybe Teri is right. Maybe relationships aren't pretty—even when you're sixteen. I could say no to the whole idea of dating Dooley. I could keep him at a distance, keep him as a friend, and make my own life a lot simpler. It's an easy word: *No.*

I remember, though, seeing an interview on television where Lennon talked about how he met Yoko. She was an artist, and she was having a showing at the Indica Gallery in London. Her exhibit was in a small white room—white walls, white carpet, white ceiling. In the center of the room was a ladder. Hanging above the ladder was a small spyglass suspended by a string. The idea was that a tiny written message awaited any viewer who took the trouble to peer through the spyglass. The visitor was then supposed to decide if the message was of value. Lennon stepped up the ladder and reached for the glass. He said later he expected the message to say *Ha! Ha!* or something crude, jabbing at him for bothering to climb the rungs. If it had, Lennon said, he would have left the museum, refusing to see the remainder of the show. Instead he stayed for all of it, and he met his future wife.

What did the message say? It was a single word.
Yes.

This Boy

☆

I'm a little nervous as I knock on Dooley's front door. I hear the stereo blaring inside—a punch of bass and a voice singing *muh-muh-muh-my Sharona*. I rap on the door, loudly, until my knuckles hurt. Dooley answers, wearing not his pajamas or sick clothes, but jeans and a long-sleeved T-shirt. His hair is mussed, but his eyes are bright and he's eating what looks like a peanut butter and banana sandwich—not at all the picture I had in my mind. With near-death images still fresh in my head, I actually feel a flash of anger toward him when I see he's not sick. He just stayed home. How dare he be well? How dare he worry me so much? I know it's perverse to be mad because your best friend is healthy, but I'm still feeling a little guilty for not coming over earlier.

And I don't *like* to feel guilty.

"Hey," he says, holding his Wonder Bread creation to my nose. "Sandwich?"

I pass on the snack, and he takes me by the hand and leads me to his room. I expect to see what I usually see—rumpled bed, clothes on the floor, maybe a cracker box or frozen food tin. I'm staggered. The room is transformed. Sure, it's still a mess, and I almost trip on a Nerf football, but Dooley's turned the place into a studio. He's pushed the bed into a corner, laid down plastic over the carpet, and opened the windows to the fall air.

"Where's your desk?" I ask.

"Corner of the living room," he says. "You missed it coming in."

He's borrowed easels from the art department at school. I count four paintings, in various stages of completion.

Rapunzel glows, her hair shimmering as she tosses it from her tower prison.

"What did you do to her?"

"Added some highlights," says Dooley.

Another painting is all browns, tans, and blacks. It's a man's face, set down in hard, jagged lines as though carved into the bark of a tree. The eyes are wide and terrified, the mouth a square, the teeth wooden.

"It reminds me of that Edvard Munch painting you once showed me," I say. "The one of the gray guy slapping his hands to his face."

"The Scream," says Dooley.

"Yeah, that one."

The third is incomplete, a background wash of color and a smear of black. I can't make anything of it. The last, I see, is *me*—my blue-white face, my straight-line smile, all those little squares that are still looking for a place to land.

"You're putting this one—me—into your show?"

"Absolutely," he says, as though other possibilities never existed.

I watch silently as he picks up a brush and deepens the color around the girl's eyes. My eyes.

So, I think, *it happens like that. Pow, you're in love.* Take that, girls. How many high school sophomores can say they have a boyfriend who's put their face in an art gallery?

"I'll take that sandwich now," I say.

He brings it to me on a paper towel, along with another for him. We sit on the edge of his bed, stare at the paintings, and feel the breeze blowing in through the open window. Outside, a little girl shrieks as she rides a tricycle. I lick peanut butter from my fingers. The Wonder Bread tastes like sponge cake.

"So, this is what you've been doing all day?"

"Yup. Wanted to work on these paintings," says Dooley. He smacks loudly, because the sandwich is sticky. A bit of bread comes out of the corner of his mouth, and I poke it back in with my finger. I get away with this intimate little gesture, but only for a moment. Dooley looks away from me. "I have to tell you something," he says.

"Hmm?"

"I'm gonna quit school."

I take the sandwich from him and set it down on the paper towel. Then I hold his hand and lay my head on his shoulder. "No, you're not," I tell him.

"I am."

"Dooley, you can't quit school. You'll lose your scholarship, remember?"

He doesn't say anything. He knows as well as I do that quitting school is a wish-list item, like heading off to Mexico for the weekend or finding a '58 Les Paul Custom at a garage sale. You think about it, it sits well in your fantasies, but you know it's not real. Dooley and I put our arms around each other, sort of rocking back and forth. It's a little motion, two or three inches forward, two or three back, and it feels nice.

"I hate them."

"I know," I say.

He means Farris Tidwell, of course, and the others. Dooley didn't have to stay home today. He could have worked on his paintings in the afternoon while I was with Teri. He has time before his exhibit. No, he stayed home because he didn't know what he would find scrawled across his locker, or on the bathroom wall, or keyed into the door of his car.

I lean up to kiss him on the cheek, and I feel his shoulders jerk slightly with surprise. He doesn't look at me, just stares out the window. I rub my thumb across the back of his hand, which feels cold. I kiss the hand. I place my head on his shoulder again. I get no response. Maybe I'm not even here. Maybe, to Dooley, the cheek-kiss was just a little wind that came up and made him shiver.

We rock some more.

"I'm not what they say," he mumbles. "I'm *not...*"

"Shhh."

I feel him shift his head to look down at me. He tries to smooth my hair from my face, a tender little gesture, but my curls tangle around a finger and he tugs too hard.

"Ow."

"Sorry...sorry." He draws his hand back and looks away.

"You all right?" I ask.

"Why?"

"I don't know. You look like your rubber band is stretched too tight or something." I laugh, but I'm only half-kidding. I can see past his eyes, and something's pinging around inside him like an overtuned guitar string. That's when he startles me. Everything is quiet, and then his face is a huge blur in front of me, his mouth landing on mine a little off center. I feel him adjust until our lips press tightly together. I feel a momentary blast of panic and suck in air through my nose. Something inside me screams to pull away, but I tell myself it's just the fact that he's surprised me. Another voice says, *It's okay. This is Dooley. You wanted this. You kissed him first.* Soon the surprise wears off, and I tell myself the kiss feels nice, but really it doesn't. It's clumsy and hard and forced, and his fingers are wrapped around my upper arms, squeezing.

I feel a noise escape from my throat: *"Mmph!"*

Dooley's weight shifts. He's over and above me, moving forward, and I have no place to go but on my back. He's on top of me, and I feel my breath punch out of my mouth and into his. He pulls away and I see his face looming over me—

"Okay, Dooley, stop—"

But he plants his lips on mine again. His tongue, tasting of peanut butter, pushes into my mouth. He makes a long noise—*mmmmmmmm*—which sounds gross and makes my stomach turn queasy. He kisses my cheek once—letting me breathe, finally, through my mouth—then moves down to my neck. My head tries to jerk back from the touch.

"Dooley," I whisper, "stop…please…?" I wedge my hands under his shoulders.

He's still making the sounds, and my throat feels cold and wet where he's kissing it. I push against his shoulders, but it's like pushing against a wall. His arms are locked around me.

"Dooley…stop it… now…okay?"

"Mmmmmmmm—"

"Dooley! I'm not kidding—"

His mouth covers mine again. Fingers wrap into a fist around the fabric of my blouse. I feel him pull, and my shirt-tail leaves my jeans. *No.* Now everything inside me screams no. He's not stopping, and I'm getting scared, and more than that I'm getting really pissed. I shove hard with both hands, throwing all my weight against him. Dooley's body pivots off me, landing him on his back. He slips off the edge of the bed, and I hear a loud thump when he hits the floor.

I'm already moving. I roll away from him, off the bed and onto the floor. I can feel my face heating up, and my hands feel shaky. One of them lands on the Nerf football, and I hurl it at him. I'm not playing. It rebounds off his forehead and does a squiggly roll out the door. Still on his butt with his legs splayed out and his arms holding him up, he stares back at me, blinking. I grab a box of Kleenex and throw it at him as hard as I can. I throw his keys at him too, because I want something he's going to *feel.* He tries to duck, and they hit his shoulder and fall, jangling, to the floor.

"Bastard!"

Dooley flinches, more so at the word than at the fact that I've tried to hurt him. His mouth is open, and he looks a little like the face in his painting, dark and carved and wounded. His arm comes up to block whatever I'm planning to throw next, but I'm out of ammunition. I scuttle backward toward the wall and hug my knees. The heat in my face is gone. My cheeks are wet, and my nose is runny. I've been crying. I'm shaking all over because my nerves are spinning out all at once.

Dooley sees the tears and starts to get up.

"Stay away from me! Just stay over there!"

He slips to the floor again, huddled at the far side of the room, silent. His eyes go vacant. He's shutting everything out—the day, the pain in his shoulder where the keys hit him, me.... At the moment I'm too pissed to care. I'm still crying as I draw myself to my feet and—one, two, three times—push my hand into the waistband of my jeans to tuck in my shirt. The Kleenex box is dented, but I rip a tissue out and blow my nose on a torn half.

"I'm leaving," I tell him.

Dooley folds himself up in the corner. He raises his head and lets it fall back against the wall, thumping it several times. The last thump is hardest, the sound noticeably sharper than the others. "You don't have to go," he says quietly. He's talking to the wall. "I'm sorry, Star. I wouldn't have hurt you. Really."

"I know, but god, Dooley, you scared the crap out of me."

I'm stuck with this stupid messy tissue, and Dooley's rearranged his whole stinking room. I find the wastebasket over by the door.

"Don't leave, okay?" He talks in this tiny, raspy voice. "I'm sorry. I'm really sorry."

"No, I better."

"Please?"

"Dooley—" I wipe my sleeve across my neck, which feels slimy from the kiss. "*Yuck.*" My lips feel puffy. "What gets into you? I mean, I don't mind kissing you. I *wanted* to kiss you. It's just that you were a little too...rough...and you scared me. And when you didn't stop—"

"I *know*..."

"So what's the matter with you?"

He closes his eyes and lets his head lean against the wall. With his tall, skinny body all folded up on the floor and his arms wrapped around his legs, he looks like a little bird, one that's clumsy and can't fly yet.

"Don't talk to me at school," I tell him. "And don't call. I need...some time."

I grab my backpack, slinging it across my shoulder, and I'm out the bedroom door. I'm halfway down the hall when I hear his voice again, a small peep from the room behind me.

"Star?"

I stop, close my eyes a second to think, and then mentally kick myself in the butt as I turn back toward him. I stand in the doorway. He still hasn't moved. "Yeah?"

He stares at my face like he looks at one of his paintings, seeing every detail. I still feel a trail of wetness across my cheek, and I swipe my hand across it.

"I'm seventeen," he says.

"Yeah, so?"

"And the other night?" he says. "When we were in the car? That was the first time any girl's ever kissed me."

I feel a little jab in my middle when he says this. I briefly envision myself walking over to him, kissing him gently on the forehead, and laying my hand on his cheek. But I can't hold onto the picture for more than a second. All I can think about, the monster idea that's charging through my mind, is that I'm too screwed up to have a boyfriend who's also a mess. Some things, I figure, you don't want to have in common.

My pack is slipping, so I hitch it up again and leave without saying a word.

12

Within You Without You

And you left?"

"Yeah. I didn't talk to him again for several days."

Dr. Artaud's pen scritches against her pad. I haven't said much. She's writing a lot. "And did…Dooley apologize?"

"Bunches of times."

"And how do you feel about it now?"

"Still mad. Not as much, though."

"Are you going to go out with him again?"

"I'm not sure."

"Why not?"

"Well, I'm not mad—anymore, I mean. I'm just not sure it's a good idea for me to hang out with someone with so many problems."

"And Dooley's problem is…?"

"He hates himself."

Scritch scritch. "It occurs to me…we've been seeing each other for a couple of months, Star, and this is the first time you've mentioned an issue involving a boy."

"I talked about Farris."

"The boy you gave a bloody nose to. I meant a romantic issue. This is the first time, right?"

I nod. I shrug. What's her point?

"Why do you think that is?" *Scritch scritch.*

"What are you writing?" I want to crane my neck, read over her shoulder.

"You're animated as you talk about Dooley."

"What's animated?"

"Well, your face is very expressive, and you gesture a lot with your hands."

"I do not."

"See? Like that."

"Oh. So?"

"So…is this boy important to you?"

"Maybe—I don't know. Yeah, kinda."

"It's okay if he is, and it's okay if he isn't. I'm just trying to get a sense of what's going on here."

"Me too," I say.

"I haven't had much opportunity to hear how you relate to male figures in your life, Star. We talk a lot about your mother. We don't talk much about your father."

"Syke is great."

"I'm not referring to Syke. I meant your biological father."

"I don't want to talk about him."

"Very well. Can you tell me why?"

"No."

"That's fine."

"I mean, I just really don't have anything to say. Mom got pregnant when she was seventeen. I don't know, my dad was just some guy who dated her for a while and then left. I was an accident."

"What did your mother say about that?"

"She told me a million times that I was a blessing."

"Did you ever ask her about your father?"

"I did when I was little. Then I stopped caring."

"Are you angry about that? About him abandoning you?"

"How would I know? I'm angry about lots of stuff. You once told me I was an anger salad."

"Point taken. So it was just the two of you—you and your mom against the world?"

"Something like that. She raised me. I went to school like every other kid. I had homework to do and chores around the house. I can't say I felt different from anyone else."

"And when you saw two-parent families together—at the mall, at the park, at a friend's birthday party—did you feel any different then? Star...?"

"Huh? Sorry, I was thinking. What was the question?"

"Did you feel any different when you saw your friends with two parents?"

"Sometimes."

"Why?"

"Listen, I said I wasn't going to talk about him. Can we change the subject?"

Scritch scritch. "Let's go back to your friend Dooley. You said he frightened you. Do you think he might hurt you? Star, why are you laughing?"

"Dooley would never hurt me. He doesn't have it in him. Instead of stepping on a bug in his apartment, he catches it and puts it outside."

"But he did frighten you. Twice now."

"Yes. Yes, he did. But I was mostly...surprised. If it had been any other guy, I would have been scared out of my mind. I'd *still* be scared."

"You see Dooley as different from other guys?"

"If you talked to him for five seconds, you wouldn't ask."

"I see. And what would I learn if I talked to him?"

"That he's basically…decent."

"And what of his other qualities?"

"He's talented. He's sensitive. He's kind. He's smart. He's deep."

"Really? And I would know all this after meeting him for five seconds?"

"Well, no…Dooley's quiet. To see all that, you'd have to know him for some time, spend day after day with him, or…"

"Or what?"

"Or look at one of his paintings."

13

Golden Slumbers

This memory is made of gold. It's all sunlight yellows.

I find my mother in the backyard. She's sitting in an automobile tire, which hangs from a tree branch by a yellow rope. Mom isn't really swinging; she just rocks back and forth, hands gripping the rope, her toe tracing a circle in the grass. We've never had a tree swing in the backyard before—just a small lawn, some prickly bushes near the fence, and a bare garden patch where she once tried to grow tomatoes but killed them by overwatering. So I'm transfixed. She makes the tire twirl slowly, the rope twisting into a braid. Then she lifts her toe from the ground, and the tire slowly spins out. Her hair is long and trails below her shoulders. A breeze catches it, blowing it across her face, briefly turning the strands into a veil. Her eyes close.

I am eight years old.

It's a summer afternoon, and I've just come from the neighbor's pool. I'm wearing a damp bathing suit—white with red and blue prancing horses. I've come home expecting to find a hot dog or two, cookies, maybe lemonade, and instead I've found my mother dangling from a tree swing.

"Mom?"

"Hey, baby."

I touch the tire, and my hand comes away dirty. It's then I see how the rubber has ground black smudges into my mom's bare legs and the seat of her cutoffs. It's just like her—to have the grand vision but miss the details, to build the tower but forget the staircase. She was so excited about building the swing she didn't bother to clean the tire first.

Her eyes are still closed. She's feeling the sun on her face.

"Aren't you afraid the rope might come loose?" I ask.

"Nope."

"How come?"

"Because," she says, "I tied it with a round turn and two half hitches."

"Huh?"

She points to the ground. Below her I see the vinyl bag that once contained the rope and with it a tattered library book: *The United States Naval Services Practical Guide to Tying Knots*. Published by the U.S. Naval Academy, forty-third edition, 1917. A square-inch-sized chunk of the jacket flakes off when I pick it up.

"Tire blew out today," she says. "Had to buy one from the used-tire dealer."

"So you made a tree swing out of the old one!"

"Yup."

"Did you make it for me?"

"I did."

"Can I get on?"

"Nope. I've decided I kind of like it. Go make your own."

"Mommm."

She laughs and presses her foot against the ground to stop the tire from turning. Slipping first one leg out and then the other, she scoops me up in her arms and guides my legs into the swing. I grip the rope and feel her fingertips gently push against my shoulder blades.

"Did you have a nice time at the party?" she asks.

"Uh-huh. I saw this boy who had a gap in his front teeth. He could spray a *lonnggg* stream of water from his mouth, like a squirt gun."

"Did he spray you?"

"Yeah, but he stopped after I snuck up behind him and pushed him into the deep end."

"Pammy!"

"I know. Mrs. Kowalski made me apologize, and I had to get out of the pool for fifteen minutes."

As I swing forward and back, the horizon moves with me. My vision fills with the green of the lawn, then green with a wide brown stripe of fence, then brown topped by blue sky, then floating puffs of white pierced by a blazing dot of sun. The colors rush by, blurring together. They halt as I reach the top of my swing, then blur again as gravity tugs me down. Without fail, at the completion of the swing's arc, I feel my mother's hands pressing into my back, sending me upward again.

"Mrs. Kowalski," I say, "is the...whaddayacallit...activities director for the recreation department."

"Yeah?"

"Yeah. She told me they were going to put on a play. About a princess and a pea or something. She said I should try out, that I would be a good princess."

The whole world is dizzying, shifting bands of green, brown, and blue. Though I can't see my mother, her presence is strong. I can hear her voice, and I can feel her hands catching me, driving me forward.

"I think you should," she says.

"Stand up on a stage in front of everybody? I'd be nervous."

"You'd like it, I bet."

"Would I have to memorize lots of lines?"

"Maybe not so many. And you'd get plenty of time to practice. I'd read them with you."

My favorite part of swinging, next to the shifting colors, is the lightheaded feeling it gives me and the roughness of the wind in my hair. I find that if I grip the rope tightly and raise my legs on the way up, I swing faster and higher. The tire presses into my skin, and the edge scratches, but I don't care. I hover at the top of my swing, hold there for the barest instant, then fall back, always—*always*—meeting the strong resistance of my mother's hands.

"Okay," I say, "maybe I will."

"That's my baby."

I keep moving up and down, my skin ice cold where the air blows through my damp swimsuit. I'm moving so fast now the colors and shapes around me become a wash: *greenbrownblue...bluebrowngreen...greenbrownblue....*

"You're swinging pretty high now. Do you want to stop?"

The tire carries me up and down three times while I consider the question. I feel it all: wind, hair, color, motion, and my mother's hands, always my mother's hands. I also feel the pull of the sky, the awareness that I could fly off the swing and land, yards away, with a broken wrist or ankle. The image is vivid. I can feel the sharp, crackling pain as strongly as I sense, behind me, my mother's firm presence. I make my decision. The next time she pushes, I hold onto the rope even more tightly and bear my weight forward, legs raised high.

"Pammy, do you want to stop?"

"No," I say. "Push harder."

Golden Slumbers

☆

It's Saturday morning. Teri Seegar stares down the neck of my mother's guitar, her eyes taking in the length of the finger-board, especially the frets.

To a guitarist like me, the little wire frets on the fingerboard are where the fingertips land; they're about the smoothness of a chord change or the amount of strength it takes to sound a note. To a luthier like Teri, frets are about even heights, smooth edges, and a good set of calipers.

"—and these frets are crap," says Teri.

"Hmm?"

I've been replacing the bridge pins on a Guild acoustic and only halfway listening. When I look up, I see Teri is now hold-ing my mother's guitar by the headstock while the body rests on her work pad. She's still peering down the neck. "Foolish to reset the neck and not do a fret job too," she says.

I put aside the guitar I'm cleaning and move next to Teri, trying to follow her gaze. All I can see is a perfectly straight neck and short, parallel lines of fret wire. "What's wrong with them?"

"Nothing but old age. Look here."

Her fingernail taps the third fret, right where the second string would cross it. Now that she's pointed, I see an obvious dip in the metal, like a mouse has taken a tiny bite from the wire.

"That's from the vibration of the string?" I ask. "It actually wears the metal away?"

"Sure. I can look at the fret wear on a guitar and tell which musical keys the owner likes to play in. Your mom was strictly D and G. Sometimes E. Looks like she didn't play in C much."

I feel a little stabbing inside me, and I force a smile to cover it up. Teri's right. Mom hated playing in C. She could never barre an F chord. "Yeah, that's Mom," I say.

"Grab that dental pick over there."

"Dental pick?"

"Nothing better for prying up a fret end, m'dear."

She shows me how to rub lemon oil into the fingerboard of the guitar to make the wood less likely to chip. Then—and I can't believe I'm doing this; it feels like murder—I begin working up the tip of each fret and tugging it out with pliers. *Gently...gently...*I warn myself. If I split the fingerboard, we're in for a whole new repair. The job is not difficult. It's just very slow, and it's against my nature to be patient. Teri hums to herself as she dusts off one guitar and replaces the strings on another.

"You love torturing me, don't you," I say. "If you were a vet, you'd probably have me doing surgery on my own puppy."

"If a guitar means a lot to you, you'll do the job right. Best way to learn."

As I work, Teri wipes down the windows with glass cleaner and vacuums the carpet, makes up her grocery list and sorts her hardware into little glass jars. She looks so innocent, but I know what's really going on. These little chores are a show, a way of sending the message that the delicate work I am doing is really simple. Window cleaning, running a vacuum, checking off the cornflakes, and fret-removal—all in a day's housework. She gives herself away, though. As she vacuums, she throws hard glances in my direction, warning me: *slowly...carefully...that's it...* She makes me nervous, but I grow into the job anyway. After a few tries, the frets pop out with ease, and I like the feel of the pick in my hand and the coolness of the wood and the way the wires clink musically when they strike the countertop.

"Teri?"

"Yeah?"

Pry. Tug. *Clink.* "Do you ever write songs to help you, y'know, work through stuff?"

"How do you mean?"

I keep my eyes down, locked on the fingerboard. I can't see anything but a stripe of rosewood, the pearl dot markers, and the faint blue background of the work pad. Sliced into the rosewood are parallel grooves where the frets once lay. They look like neat little scars.

"Like when your mom died. Did you write a song about her?"

I had been hearing a rubbery squeak as Teri wheeled the vacuum cleaner back into its corner. Now the squeaking stops. "Yeah," she says. "I tried."

"Did you finish it? Was it good?"

She laughs. "No, it pretty much stank like a wet dog."

We don't talk for a while. Now that I've finished removing the frets, Teri has to take over the more delicate job of tapping in the new ones. It's precise, almost surgical work.

"This is one of those jobs you have to mess up eight or ten times before you start getting it perfect," she says.

"Why not just pound the fret in as far as it will go?" I suggest.

"Bad idea. You'll drive it in too deep."

"What happens then?"

She stares down the neck, blowing away a bit of sawdust. "You start over, hon."

Teri spends another two hours leveling and dressing the frets, gently filing until all the wires are the exact same height. She uses a recrowning file to round off any flat edges. It's all filing, smoothing, and wiping now. The frets glisten.

"Would you play it for me?" I ask.

"Hmm?"

"The song you wrote for your mother. I'd like to hear it. Play it on the little parlor guitar." I wipe away the fret filings with a damp cloth, and I brush them from the work pad with my fingers.

"Ah, I don't think that's a very good idea."

"Why not?"

"You'll get a tune in your head—or a lick. You'll like it, but it won't be yours."

"But—"

She raises her hand, shushing me. "You've got to find your own song, Star," she says. "Mine'll just mess with your head."

She plants her elbows on the counter and rests her chin in her palms. I do the same, and together we stare at my mother's guitar. The neck is perfect, the joint solid and invisible. The gaping crack along the edge is now a hairline that vanishes into the grain of the wood. The braces underneath are solid. The new frets and tuning machines shine like jewelry.

"I can't believe it," I say. "It's finally finished."

I'm looking at this guitar in front of me, and I wonder—what exactly is this thing? What's inside staring back? It's beautiful and clean and...alive in a way, since it was made from living trees. I get a frightening feeling that I owe it something. I don't mean the basic responsibilities—caring for the wood, changing the strings, playing it. The guitar seems to be demanding something more. I'm supposed to *know* it. I'm supposed to know the roundness of the neck like I know my own arm. I'm supposed to know the length of a note's sustain and the hand strength it takes to bend a string up one half tone in pitch. The guitar is challenging me to discover chords I've never known, to play licks I've never tried. I can't breathe. Part of me wants to jump up and down. Another part wants to run.

"She's ready now, isn't she," I say. "All we have to do it put strings on her and tune her up."

"Not yet," says Teri.

I look again at the guitar. The repairs are solid. The adhesives have dried. The frets are perfect. It's ready.

"I don't understand."

Teri gives me one of her evil smiles. "Do you trust me?"

Later, I'm in my bedroom at home. I'm flat on my back, staring at the ceiling, and my Telecaster sits on its stand untouched. The tape in my player came to the end of side A several minutes ago. I remember hearing a brief hiss from the leader tape followed by a click. I have to force myself to stay on the bed. I want to throw in another tape or crank up the radio, maybe fire up the Tele and play a few power chords. It would feel good just to scream. I want noise to drown out the crummy thoughts that creep around in the silence—the ones that scream at me that I'm all alone and that I'll never see my mother again.

The stereo is in the corner. *Just slip off the bed. Turn the tape over. Punch* Play. *Rock your world.*

I stay where I am. I *make* myself stay.

Syke's been on the phone for half an hour. I've been lying here, listening to the dull murmur of his voice. The first call came from my grandmother. I know she wants me to come up for a visit, but I don't want to...not yet. Syke backed me up. Sometimes the pitch of his voice would peal upward, and I could hear him say her name. Other times it was a low rumble, like a thunderstorm that's far away but coming. I clearly heard the slam of the phone against its cradle when the call ended. Now I don't know who's on the line. I just hear Syke's voice rattling off short phrases, which are followed by very long silences. He's asking questions, and I guess the answers are coming in paragraphs. When the conversation is over, I hear his footsteps thudding down the hallway toward my room. My door is open, and he raps on the frame with his thick knuckle.

"Hey," I say.

"Hey there. I'm off the phone now. Thought I better tell you that your friend called earlier. You weren't home from the guitar shop."

Dooley. I haven't spoken to him in over a week, dodging him at school and not answering when he called. "N'kay. Who were you talking to?"

Syke runs his hand over his goatee as though it itches, but I think he's just buying time, trying to decide how much he wants to say. "A few people. Your grandparents. My supplier was late again, so I called to give him a piece of my mind."

"And who after that?"

"Mike. I called to apologize for blowing up at him the other day." He sniffles self-consciously. "And then I called Dr. Artaud."

I sit up, pull a pillow against my stomach, and hug it. "How come?"

"Just to talk. After the other day, I was thinking that maybe it wouldn't hurt for me to see her too. She was saying it might even be good for you and me to have a session together now and then. You okay with that?"

When I hear this, the center of my chest turns warm, and I have the sensation of something drawing me upward. The feeling makes me almost uncomfortable, so I shift around so that I'm sitting perfectly straight. "Sure—sure. I think it's a great idea. Are we...I mean, can we talk about her now?"

Syke waits before answering. His hand does a little flip of agreement. "Um...yeah, go ahead."

I wasn't expecting this moment. If I had known it was coming right now, I would have made some notes or something. I've been wanting to talk with Syke about Mom ever since she died. We never have, and I talk to Dr. Artaud instead, but it's not the same. Syke knows me, and he knows stuff about how I feel that Dr. Artaud can't know. Sure, she's read about it in a book, or studied it in a college class, or listened to another client talk about it. But book knowledge isn't good enough. Unless you've stood next to the coffin, everything else is second-hand news.

Still, I start with what she taught me: "Do you get...mad at Mom? For dying, I mean?"

He nods. "Do you?"

"Yeah. All the time. It's like, she's supposed to help me pick out a wedding dress when I get married, and now she can't. She's supposed to talk to me about the best brand of disposable diapers when I have my first kid. She's supposed to take pictures of me and my date on prom night."

Syke perks up at this. "Well, I can take pictures, for crying out loud." Now I've insulted his manly sense of competence.

"Yeah," I say, "but prom's a girl thing. You'll hold the camera, but you won't *get* it. And I'm trying not to be pissed about it, but I am."

Syke accepts this. His eyes drop, and for a moment I swear I can see the movies running through his mind, all the stuff *he* had planned to do with my mom. The vacations. Family get-togethers. A million Christmases. Still holding hands in their seventies. He rubs his eyes and leans against the doorframe, letting it bear some of his weight. His shoulders slump. I spend so much energy on my own battles—with school, Dooley, Dr. Artaud—I sometimes forget Syke is in charge of the whole war. He lost my mom. He deals with my craziness. He fights his own inner demons. Now all of the effort shows. I never thought he looked old before.

Then he undoes it all with a simple grin. "Feel better?"

I nod.

"Homework done?"

"Yup."

"Okay. Call your friend. Lights out at eleven, understand?"

I salute. I'm not giving Syke any lip. Tonight he's my hero.

When he leaves, I reach for the princess phone by my bed and punch in Dooley's number. I hesitate before hitting the last button, because I'm not really sure I want to talk to him. In my mind I see his face, the way he looked when I left his apartment a week ago. I remember his long body huddled on the floor, collapsed in on itself. Now I'm shaking my head at my own stupidity. This is just *great*. I'm still angry, and I'm still feeling sorry for the guy. These emotions I can understand. But the overriding feeling I have—the one that really has me flummoxed—is that I just really like the guy. I miss him. I *want* to call him. Tomorrow, I remember, his paintings will go up in the Spectrum Gallery, framed and ready for the one-week exhibit that will begin Saturday. Dooley was even featured in the morning announcements that come over the closed-circuit television at school, so everyone heard about his success. Two days ago, as I was heading for the bus after school, I saw a student reporter pointing a camera at Dooley, catching him unaware. Dooley sat hunched under our oak tree, his hands moving like dancers around a sheet of paper, folding, folding.

Still, before I punch in the last number, I clamp my thumb

down on the disconnect button. I can't talk to him. Not tonight. My head is filled with a wild, swirling tornado. I envision my mother's guitar, and I feel that weight pressing on me again: I have yet to write her song. I see Syke, his finger tapping a tower made of glass bottles. I see my grandmother and a bedroom in Vermont decorated with plush toys and painted in pink, the one color I cannot tolerate. I see my teachers, one by one, as they point to their gradebooks—and to the empty spaces that line up beside the name "Cochran, Pamela Jean." I see the black glass window of the ISS room, the name "Jon" etched into it with silver light. I grow more and more tired.

Talk to Dooley? Maybe tomorrow. Maybe next week.

I slip off the bed and walk over to my makeup table. Fumbling, I reach for my mother's letter to John Lennon, which stands upright against the mirror, and for my ticket to the Elton John concert. I bring both back to my bed. I lie down, draw the covers around me, and hold them against my chest, eyes closed. My legs and arms feel heavy, my eyes feel tired and dry, and for a few moments I just want to rest. I want to pretend for one night that nobody needs me and nothing is pulling at me—not school, not Dooley, not Syke, not even my mother. Because I can't handle it. I just can't handle it. I don't even have the energy to cry.

It's something like six-thirty at night, and dark enough outside to make me sleepy in spite of all the noise in my head. Without opening my eyes, I set the ticket and the letter on my bed table and switch off my lamp. The room goes black. My mind grows quieter. Syke hasn't turned on the television yet, and I can't hear him in the kitchen. My last thought, one that makes me smile just before I fall asleep, is that the silence around me isn't so frightening after all. It's wonderful.

14

While My Guitar Gently Weeps

School feels strange without Dooley. I've been avoiding the oak tree in the morning, taking a longer walk around the building and using a side entrance instead of the front. I've stayed away from the art department and away from his locker. At lunchtime I've gone to the cafeteria's outside counter, grabbing my meal and eating it by the chain-link fence along the edge of the baseball field. I've seen his blue Gremlin in the parking lot, but I haven't gone near it.

He could come to me, of course. He could meet me at my locker between classes; he knows my schedule as well as I do. He could look for me at lunch. He could leave his sixth-period class early, claiming he needed to use the restroom, and be waiting for me by the door of my sixth period when the bell rang. A little move like that would be *romantic*. Now I'm driving myself crazy. I tell myself I don't want the hassle of a boyfriend. I tell myself that the silence I heard last night, the rest and the peace that came with it, was a sign that I need time alone. Still, none of that would matter if Dooley were to suddenly appear at my side and lay his arm across my shoulder. At that moment, all my conflicted feelings would be like beach sand washing away under my feet. Nothing. But I don't expect my little fantasy to come true. Dooley thinks I've rejected him, and he doesn't like himself enough to believe I'd give him another chance.

I muddle through math. I write poetry in my journal instead of doing the grammar worksheet in English. In history I draw an Afro hairdo on a picture of King Charles III.

When the bell rings ending the school day, I head for my locker. First, though, I peer around the corner to see if Dooley is waiting for me. He's not, and I'm a little miffed. I spin the combination dial angrily, tug on the handle a little too hard.

And when I yank open the door, a dozen red roses land at my feet.

The hallway is crowded, and I hear gasps from one or two other girls. I bend down to touch one of the roses and find that it's made of paper—red construction paper, folded and refolded on itself to form layers of curled petals. An origami bouquet. The flower stems are black tissue paper rolled around lengths of old bass guitar strings. I sniff them. He's scented each one—not with rose scent, but with some kind of cheesy aftershave. I laugh. The red is beautiful, sharp enough to catch the eye and soft enough to seem natural. The black is…well, the black is just Dooley.

I'm still holding one of the roses when I arrive at Teri's shop. I twirl it between my fingers. I sniff it. I slip it into a buttonhole near the collar of my Levi's jacket and go right to work.

"Okay," I say after half an hour, "when do I get to see it?"

My mother's guitar is nowhere to be seen, and Teri still hasn't mentioned it.

"Hmm?"

"The Gibson. May I see it?"

"Oh, sure," she says. "Whenever you'd like. Would you do me a favor and vacuum the front? I've been swamped all day."

She smiles as she says this. The front doesn't look all that bad, but clearly Teri is plotting something, and I figure it won't hurt me to play along. I vacuum without complaint. I vacuum with diligence. The carpet in the front is a spotless emerald color when I'm finished.

"Great," says Teri. "The sink in back is dirty."

"Teri, this is psychological torture."

Her light Texas accent turns thick as molasses when she answers. "Hon, I'm just a guitar-picker from Austin. I don't know nothin' 'bout no psychologicals."

I sigh and scrub the stupid sink.

She plays me this way for the remainder of the afternoon. I put new tuners on a Takamine twelve-string, then take a throw rug outside and shake it until the dust makes me cough. I reglue a loose bridge plate on a Fender and rinse down the outside of the shop windows with a bucket of water and a squeegee. For the entire two hours, I am both craftsman and janitor.

"May I see my mother's guitar now?"

Teri glances at the open door of the restroom in the back, specifically at the commode inside.

"Okay, okay," I tell her. "I'll scrub the toilet. Just don't do the accent anymore."

A little before six she sends me for sandwiches. We sit together on a little grassy patch just outside the shop, where we watch the people and the traffic.

"Shouldn't we be inside?" I ask. "In case a customer comes?"

She shrugs. "Anyone going in will have to walk right past us, and we're close enough to hear the phone."

She's right, but I still feel odd sitting here. We've never done this before.

While My Guitar Gently Weeps

Teri doesn't speak, so I just sip my blue raspberry Slurpee and wait. The boulevard, this time of evening, is a stream of cars three lanes wide in both directions. They move together, clogging the intersections each time the lights turn from yellow to red. A huge diesel truck spews a plume of black smoke and makes a loud, foghorn bellow. At the bus stop, a child cries.

"'Beautiful noise,'" says Teri.

"Hmm?"

"It's an old song." She nods toward the street. "Hear it? Traffic, car horns, kids shouting—it's all music. Beautiful noise. You find good songs in the simple stuff. Pick your favorite song, Star, and look at the lyrics. I'd be willing to bet it doesn't talk about feelings. It gives you images—something to see, something to hear, something to smell."

I nod. I'm watching the sun set behind an old brick building. Soot peppers the building's walls and blackens the window frames. "You know," I say, "I miss the beach. I used to go there at sunset, sit on the lifeguard stand, and play my guitar. I haven't gone in a while."

"Remember what the surf sounds like?"

"Sure."

"Tell me."

I can't answer right away. I have to close my eyes and think about it. I feel the wooden slats of the lifeguard stand underneath me. I can see the sun, huge in the distance, its light a warm reddish orange. I see the boats of the marina. I hear the waves...

"Okay. It's like...like...a huge wind takes a step toward you and then walks away."

I open my eyes and see Teri looking back at me. "That's good," she says. "That's pretty good." She crumples the bag her sandwich came in and tosses it into a trash can. Then she dusts off her hands and pushes herself up from the grass. "Come on. Let's go look at your guitar."

When we're back in the work area, she heads toward a metal cabinet, which she unlocks with a key. Inside is a guitar case, but it looks nothing like my mother's. It's new, high-impact plastic, arch-topped, unbreakable. "The case is a gift," says Teri. "My way of saying happy birthday to a new songwriter."

"Today's not my birthday."

"I *know*. I mean a new *songwriter* is born today. Geez, Star, let me have my fun." She sets the case on her workbench and shifts it around so the latches face me. "You'll want to keep the old battered one, since it's the original that came with the guitar, but this is the one you should use."

I rub my hand along the outside of the case. It feels hard and a little rubbery. The latches are heavy and stiff. When I pop one, I hear a little poof of air. The others behave the same, snapping smartly when I touch them, and in a moment all I have to do is raise the lid.

Which I do.

"Star?"

"Wait, wait," I whisper. "I have to breathe."

The guitar is...astounding. Polished. Clean. Magical. The finish catches the light from Teri's work lamp and throws it against the wall in front of me, making a patch of amber that slips and slides as I lift the guitar from the case. She's put on a brand-new set of phosphor-bronze strings, which look like pure gold against the dark wood.

"You've been calling it your mother's guitar," says Teri. "I wanted to make it your own."

It's then I see what she's done. She's removed the old pearl dots that marked the frets. She's replaced all of them. No more dots. No more any-old-guitar. The fingerboard of the Gibson, *my* Gibson, now glistens with a sprinkling of stars.

☆

That night at home, I play it for the first time. I tried to play it in Teri's shop, but I couldn't. I wanted so much for her to see how grateful I felt, and the best way to do that, I know, would have been to let her hear me play. I really tried. I imagined myself running through some bluesy lick, impressing her with my skill. She might even have picked up one of the other guitars and played along, throwing some lead around my rhythm.

Here's how it went instead: I sat on her metal stool, held the guitar against me, and strummed a simple chord. The moment I heard that bright, jangly sound—the sound I heard so often behind my mother's voice—I had to stop. The chord rang out stupidly, until every note decayed to silence, because I didn't think to mute the strings. I just started crying. Now, I cried in the days leading up to my mother's death. I cried at her funeral. I cried in the days that came after, especially when I felt alone or when the night seemed particularly dark. As a child I was afraid of the dark, and my mother used to come and sit on the edge of my bed and whisper to me. After she died, nighttime became almost unbearable.

I have to say, though, that I have never cried like I did at the moment my pick hit those strings. I understand how a guitar produces sound: Strings vibrate. Wood resonates. But I guess something inside a person resonates too. I heard that chord, and every memory of my mother seemed layered on top of the sound, like harmonics. So I bawled. Not just tears—these were loud sobs that made my stomach muscles ache. I felt Teri slip the guitar from my lap and rest her arm across my shoulders.

I leaned my head against her and cried myself out. I have no idea how long she held me, what she said, or if she said anything at all. I just remember the feel of her shoulder against my cheek and, after a while, a gentle motion as she rocked me slightly back and forth. Several minutes passed before I could speak.

"I miss her so much," I said.

"I know, hon."

As she held me, Teri didn't feel at all like my mother. Mom was shorter than Teri, and her round figure made her softer to the touch. Teri is all straight lines. Also, Mom's hair was fine and wavy, so Teri's red, steel wool hair felt wrong, too, as it brushed my forehead. The light scent of her clothing was different, as was the weight of her arms and the strength of her hug. Still, I held on to her like someone hanging over the edge of a cliff holds onto the last little tree branch or root.

That was hours ago. Now it's late. I've been lying in bed since nine, and my clock reads minutes past midnight. My precious Telecaster rests in its case, which I've shoved to the back of my closet. The Gibson now sits on my bedroom guitar stand. I can see it in the shadows, and I know I have to play. I'm pretty sure I'm ready. I slip from the covers and reach for it, fumbling at the same time for one of the picks that always seem to gather on my nightstand. I sit on the edge of my bed, hold the guitar to me, and just wait there a moment. I wrap my arms around it, hugging it, getting used to the weight and the shape and, most importantly, to the way it makes me feel.

Then I strum a chord. Mute the strings. Close my eyes. Breathe.

The sound and the feelings are the same as they were in Teri's shop, but this time I'm ready. My eyes warm, and one tear makes a trail down my cheek, but I just wipe it away with my hand and play another chord. Just a chord. I know my limits. A moment later I try some fingerpicking, just two bars of "Julia," and I can tell I've pushed myself too far. My mother's letter to John Lennon stares back at me from my dressing table.

Mute the strings...close your eyes...breathe...

Over the next twenty minutes I start to understand the layers a little better, all the feelings that piled on top of one another when I tried to play earlier. This sounds weird, but so much of my mother seems to live in this guitar. I've kept a lot of her belongings, and sometimes a piece of her clothing or jewelry will light up some weird old memory I haven't thought of in years. Happens all the time. The guitar, I sense, is something even more powerful. Holding it, hearing it the way it sounded when she played, makes me hear her voice as well. Hearing her voice makes me see her face. Seeing her face makes me feel her touch—like the way her lips felt moist on my forehead when she kissed me good night. Feeling her touch brings on smells—the shampoo in her hair, the fabric softener in her blouse. The images pile up, layer upon layer. Notes ringing above notes. Harmonics. The longer I play, the more overwhelming her presence is. I feel a ball of warmth in the middle of my chest that keeps growing and radiating. I feel...safe. And loved. I'm not really paying much attention to what I'm playing, to where my fingers land on the neck. I'm just living inside this feeling, whatever it is, for as long as it will let me.

After a while the warmth fades. I look at the clock and realize I've been playing for forty minutes. A voice inside me says *Put the guitar away now. You're tired.* And so I do. I set it on its stand and crawl back into bed.

For a long time, I just stare at it.

15

Nowhere Man

So I'm nuts, right?"

Dr. Artaud doesn't think my question is very funny. She leans forward in her chair and tips her head down, studies me over the lenses of her glasses. I wonder if it would hurt her to smile at my little joke, and then I realize, just as quickly, that she probably didn't hear it as a joke.

And maybe, just maybe, I didn't really mean it as one.

"Do *you* think you're nuts?" she asks.

"You're the one with all the letters after your name."

"Point taken." She makes a notation on her pad—pauses, frowns, starts to write again—but then lets the pen clatter to her desktop and pushes the pad away. "Star, when a young person loses a parent, it's not unusual for objects to take on a...a special significance. Your mother owned the guitar; it was important to her. You're a musician, playing guitar is a huge part of who you are, so it's only natural that this particular object would have an effect on you. By that I mean a much greater effect than, say, a piece of clothing or jewelry. So yes, what you felt was perfectly normal—and no, you are not nuts."

Everything she says makes perfect sense. She has years of

education, years of experience, to prepare her for the moment
I walked through her door today. She has wisdom and common sense. She has a natural gift for understanding how her
patients feel at a given moment. She is a careful listener. As a
therapist, Dr. Artaud has many talents, so I listen to her
politely and bite my tongue to keep from telling her she's full
of crap. Last night, when I held that guitar, I *felt* something. I
wasn't reminiscing. I wasn't dreaming. I wasn't imagining.

"Anything else?"

I shake my head.

"Okay. How is your friend Dooley?" she asks.

"He's probably going a little crazy himself. The gallery is
bringing in his paintings tonight to get them ready for the
exhibition."

"This is a big deal for him."

"Absolutely."

"Will you be attending?"

I close my eyes and let out a little *shoof* of breath. I've been
dreading this question.

I've come to the realization that the situation with Dooley is
hopeless. I'd like him to call, but I doubt he will. I'd like to be
his guest the night of the opening, but I doubt he'll ask. His
feelings are too hurt. I figure that over time we'll likely be
friends again—we're too close to stay apart for very long—but
I think Dooley has written off the idea that I could be his girl-
friend. He won't call because he thinks I'll hurt him again.
And I won't call because—well, darn it, I want *him* to call *me*.

"Star, do you think Dooley is gay?"

The question catches me by surprise, and I laugh. "I can
pretty much vouch that he isn't."

"Perhaps your friend is afraid that you think he might be
gay, so he's trying overly hard to prove to you he isn't."

Pepperland

I nod. Dr. Artaud hasn't told me anything I haven't figured out for myself, but it still doesn't get me any closer to what I want—which is to hear from Dooley. I'm starting to realize that I might just have to cave in on this one and make the call first.

The doctor consults her little pad again. Not only does she write down notes about every little word I utter, she also appears to keep her own little agenda for our meetings. "Another thing, Star. I've noticed lately that you seem calmer, more focused, and—if I dare say so—even a little happier."

I smile, covering my mouth with my hand as I do. I haven't told Dr. Artaud about my plans to meet John Lennon, to talk to him and give him my mother's letter. The idea sounds crazy even to me, and I can only imagine the pages upon pages of dire notes she would be scribbling after I left her office if I told her. Really, it's about the only thought in my head that I've kept to myself. It feels private—and to be honest, I kind of enjoy keeping a secret from her.

"I guess you could say I have a mission."

"Missions can be good," she says. She picks up her pen again, taps it on the pad as she waits for me to say more.

I don't.

That night I try, once again, to write my mother's song. I'm tired, and it's late, but a full moon sends a bright, bluish light through my window and makes it hard for me to sleep. The Gibson sits there, only steps away. I kick off the covers and reach for it, then bring it to bed with me and sit up with pillows piled against my back. I've been playing it daily, and I'm getting better with it. I can strum through entire songs now without falling apart. Instead of steeling myself against a flood of emotion, I find I can listen to the guitar and love it just for its sound. The old wood darkens the tone, and it seems to sing best when I play hard. I feel comfortable holding it, as though my body were designed to nestle against this particular guitar, and this one only.

But when I try to play something for my mom, nothing comes. I can play anything, the most difficult pieces I know, but the door slams in my face when I try to come up with something for her. I play, I noodle around, and then I give up. Yawning, I place the guitar back on its stand and enjoy looking at it until I drift off to sleep.

Hours later, the phone jangles me awake.

It rings twice, three times before my fumbling hand finds it. My bedside clock tells me it's just past one A.M., and I feel a jolt. Who would call at this hour? I imagine an emergency room call from my grandmother: My grandfather's had a heart attack or an accident. Someone's broken into their home, or there's been a fire.

Or it's Dooley.

"Hullo?"

"Star Cochran?"

It's a woman's voice. I don't recognize it, but I hear a little hitch in her breathing, like she's terribly upset and trying not to cry.

"Yeah…yeah, that's me. Who is this?"

"Miss Cochran, I'm sorry to be calling so late. My name is Suzanne Cohen. I'm the owner of the Spectrum Gallery. Something…well…something terrible has happened, and Sean O'Doul has asked me to call you."

"Sean…? *Dooley?* What happened?"

"I know this is troubling. There's been some…some…it's just terrible."

"Is he hurt?"

"No, but…"

In the background I hear Dooley's voice. It sounds high-pitched and desperate. "Ask her if she can come here. Tell her I need her *here*."

"He wants to know if you can—"

"I'll be there in twenty minutes."

I say this without thinking, and I hang up the phone without correcting myself. It's only as I'm throwing on clothes that I consider the possibility that Syke might have something to say about my leaving the house in the middle of the night. I think. I weigh options. He's probably not awake. Syke sleeps like an old dog, and I doubt he even heard the phone. If I wake him and ask for permission to leave, he'll say no. Actually, he'll say "Are you out of your mind? Go back to bed." So I don't wake him. I dig through the jacket he left on the living room coatrack until I find the keys to his truck.

Three police cruisers, with lights flashing, sit in the parking lot of the Spectrum Gallery. I see a cop standing over three shadowy figures. They huddle on the ground with their arms locked behind them, and it's clear they're in handcuffs. I can't see their faces, only black shapes, until I move past them. The glow of the gallery's sign turns orange on the faces of three boys. Two I recognize from school, though I don't know their names. They stare past the cop, their faces like the masks in the hallway of the art department at school, flat and expressionless, mouths like straight lines. The third has turned his face toward the ground. Filthy brown hair tips forward, covering his eyes. He hears my shoes making a rubbery sound against the pavement, and his head tilts up. Eyes set too closely together look back at me from beneath the hair. The face is round and doughy, covered with acne scars. Farris Tidwell and I stare at each other. He whispers "bitch," and the cop tells him to shut up.

Farris. Oh, God.

I rush past them, but another cop at the entrance stops me. I tell him my name, and he waves me in. "Stay away from there," he says, pointing. Before me is the main display area of the gallery, filled with modern paintings and a strange bronze sculpture the size of a refrigerator. The cop is indicating an exhibit room off to my left, now blocked by crossing strips of neon yellow crime scene tape. Hoping to find Dooley, I walk over and peer inside.

Four police officers collect evidence. They brush black dust everywhere, seeking fingerprints. Another uses a large sheet of transparent material to lift a shoe print. I see red. I see red *everywhere*. Three one-gallon paint cans rest on the marble floor, dripping red. Red spatters mar the walls. A red slash mark cuts across the ceiling. Blood-red letters, each the length of my arm, drip and run like letters in the title of a horror movie. They cover Dooley's paintings, obliterating them. Six paintings, six letters to spell out a word.

F-A-G-G-O-T.

My stomach shrinks inside me and tries to crawl up my throat. I wrap my arms around my middle and lean against the doorframe because my knees have gone weak. I just stand there and watch, not knowing where to go or what to do, and I start to cry for Dooley.

"Miss Cochran?"

The light and whispery voice comes from just over my left shoulder. The woman standing behind me is shorter than I am and has frizzy, salt-and-pepper hair that seems to fly in every direction. She wears pointy cat's-eye glasses. Her nose is red because, like me, she's been crying.

"I'm Star."

"I'm Suzanne." She gazes past me into the room and shakes her head. "I've had this gallery for twelve years. Never has anyone done anything this cruel and stupid."

"Where's Dooley? Is he all right?"

She points down a dark, narrow hallway. I find Dooley at the end of it. He's sitting on the floor, his back against the wall and his knees drawn up. He stares into empty space. As I draw closer, I see that his eyes are red, though he doesn't appear to be crying. I slip down next to him and take one of his hands in mine. I lightly rub my finger over his knuckles, which I see are swollen and bruised.

"Let me guess," I whisper. "You got mad and punched the wall."

"Three times," he says.

I want to yell at him, but I let it go. If I were in his place, I might have bruised my knuckles too. "So tell me what happened."

"Ooh. Let me see. Well, Farris and his weasely little buddies broke into the gallery and trashed my art. Like the idiots they are, they didn't realize they'd set off a silent alarm. The alarm company called the police, the police called the owner, and the owner called me. The police busted them while they still had the brushes in their hands."

"How bad is it?"

He sniffles, then shrugs. "Bad enough. Most of the art was behind glass, but the paint seeped past the glass and into the frame. I might be able to save one or two of those by trimming half an inch or so around the edges. They broke the glass on two of the pieces, slashed the art. The Rapunzel was in a wood frame—no glass. It's ruined...gone."

We lean into each other, tipping our heads so they touch. Dooley's grip on my hand grows tighter. "Don't go away, all right?"

"I'm here."

A long time passes. We don't say anything. We just sit, our hands wrapped together, our heads touching, our bodies swaying just the tiniest bit. The moment feels *nice*. I know that's an odd word, considering the circumstances, but it's how I feel. "You know what?" I say. "I don't get you."

"What do you mean?"

I squiggle my body so we're even closer. "I don't know...they trashed your art, painted that word all over your exhibit. I figured you'd be crazed. I'd expect you to be crying, or pounding your head against the wall. If nothing else, I figured you'd be out in the parking lot trying to kill Farris."

Dooley traces his index finger along the back of my hand. I'm tingling.

"I'm smart, and they're not," he says. "I can paint, and they can't. I'm better than they are, and they can't stand it." My words. Dooley remembered them. He leans into me and kisses me on the cheek. "I'm glad you're here."

Mrs. Cohen comes down the hallway. She takes off her glasses, wipes her eyes, blows her nose into a rumpled Kleenex she pulls from her coat pocket. "I'm so sorry," she says. "You still have the scholarship, Sean. And we can put the exhibition off for another month." Behind her a blue light pulses against the walls. It's the light from the police cars outside.

"Why are they still here?" I ask, meaning Farris and his friends. "Why aren't their asses already in jail?"

"They weren't carrying any identification," she explains,

"and at first they refused to give their names to the police. I called Sean because I thought...I thought he might know them. Don't worry. The police are taking them away now."

I haul myself to my feet and tug on Dooley's hand. "Come on," I say. "I'll take you home."

He waves an arm in the general direction of the parking lot. "I have my car."

"Yeah, well, you don't need to be driving. Tomorrow's Saturday. We'll come back for your car."

I lead him to Syke's truck. His legs seem a little unsteady under him, so I stay close, his arm over my shoulder. "Come on. Get in." Our drive to his apartment is silent. He stares out the window, occasionally raising his head and letting it fall back against the glass. For me, the trip is all hazy lights—neon signs on storefronts, street lamps, and stoplights blending together. When we arrive at his apartment, I guide him up the staircase. His elbow hits the wrought iron rail, and it clangs and hums. Dooley doesn't react. I discover something: He left in such a hurry the door is not even fully closed. I touch it, and it swings open into a dark living room. The TV set flickers— some kind of black-and-white gangster movie with the volume turned low.

"Hey," I whisper, "how come your mom isn't up waiting for you? Isn't she all panicked that you left in the middle of the night?"

"Huh-uh. She got home around ten, took a Valium, and went straight to bed. She won't be conscious until morning."

I turn off the TV and lead Dooley into his room. He collapses on the bed. His eyes close almost instantly. I sit on the edge, and while his breathing becomes less ragged, I quietly tug off his shoes and socks. It feels like an intimate, wifely sort of gesture, and I like doing it. Dooley opens his eyes and smiles.

"Thank you."

I lie down next to him, rub my hand along his cheek. "You're welcome. Are you going to be all right?"

"I'll make it."

"I guess that's as positive as any of us can be, considering."

I take both of Dooley's hands in mine and raise them over his head. We lock our fingers together, we squeeze, we run our thumbs lightly back and forth. Our noses nearly touch, and I hardly have to move at all to kiss him. He's too tired and shell-shocked to get all tense on me, so the kiss is actually pretty nice—short and sweet enough to make me want to kiss him again.

So I do.

"I've been wondering," he says, "about your plan. You're still going through with it, right? You're going to the concert, and you're going to try to give your mom's letter to John Lennon?"

"Absolutely. It's coming up in a few days, and Lennon's definitely going to be doing a guest shot. They've been talking about it on the radio all week."

"Yeah," says Dooley, "I heard. I've been thinking, and you know what? It's kind of like you're making a trip to Pepperland."

"Pepperland?"

"Did you ever see *Yellow Submarine?* That animated Beatle movie?"

I remember something from when I was a little girl—bright colors, cartoon Beatles, strange animals. "I think so," I say. "My mom took me to see it when I was, like, five."

"Yeah, that'd be it. Pepperland was the magic place the Beatles went to, okay? And they had to fight these monsters called the Blue Meanies. That's what you're doing. You're fighting off the Blue Meanies. You're going to Pepperland."

"You're sweet."

We kiss some more, and as we're kissing, I slowly draw one of his hands down—past my cheek, past my shoulder, where it hangs for a moment nervously—and I place it on my breast. My hand stays on top of his, keeping him settled, preventing him from getting clumsy and rough.

"I'm going to lay down three rules, okay?" I tell him.

"Okay."

We kiss again. "Rule number one is, the clothes stay on, got it?"

"Uh-huh."

More kissing. Longer this time. "Rule number two is, hands stay outside the clothing."

"Would that be all clothing," asks Dooley, "or just under-clothes?"

I laugh. "*All* clothes, beanhead. This isn't a negotiation."

The conversation sort of dies out there. Dooley is too exhausted to be anything but relaxed. I feel a little panic now and then while we're kissing, but it's not about Dooley. I'm imagining Syke pacing the front yard at home, his eyes smoldering at the thought that I'm not in my room and his truck is not in the driveway. Having noted the feeling, however, I very quickly get distracted from it.

"Hey..." Dooley says a while later.

"Hey what?"

"You never told me number three."

"Hmm?"

"Rule number three. You never told me what it was." He kisses my neck.

"Oh, hell," I say, "I forget number three."

16

Imagine

Lennon's coming. He's coming tonight, and my fingers can't seem to get the button through the buttonhole on my Levi's. My favorite top makes the skin on my back and shoulders itch. A little pink pimple, sore to the touch, sits right next to my nose. Nothing feels right because I'm stressing. And I'm stressing because tonight, in just a few hours, *he's* coming.

I've showered three times today. Once before school, a second time because I stank after gym class, and a third time when I got home, just to be safe. You don't mess around when you're heading off to meet a former Beatle.

My clock says 5:17. I'm standing in front of a full-length mirror, turning my head this way and that, checking out my hair. I had thought about talking Dooley into cutting sixth period with me, driving me home so I could get a head start on my look, but then I realized too much primping might be dangerous. A low-cut blouse, a high-cut skirt, a knockout hairdo might get me noticed by a backstage roadie—which is precisely the idea—but I might just as easily catch the eye of a security guard. A frumpy sweatshirt and ponytail would help me blend in, but they wouldn't be—let's be honest—sexy enough to keep that same roadie from tossing me out on my rear. I'm not going to sell myself out to meet John Lennon, but

Pepperland

I'm not above a little manipulation as long as it doesn't go beyond a sleazy look or two. I decide on a style somewhere in-between: jeans tight enough to look good, a blouse that's eye-catching but not too clingy, hair blown dry and brushed out straight. I give myself a last check. The outfit is perfect. Chances are a guy would look at me; he just wouldn't look *twice*.

I hear a knock from the doorway behind me. Syke stands there, his hand self-consciously gripping his wallet. "The truck is gassed up. Um, here," he says. He slips a twenty and a ten from the wallet and sets them on my makeup table. "Some emergency cash, or in case you want to buy, I don't know, a T-shirt or something. Sure you don't want me to drive you?"

"Nah, I'll be fine." I give him a big hug. "Thank you, though." Next he gets a sloppy kiss on the cheek.

I know why I'm being so loving toward him. It's partly because Syke is so kind and generous. Mostly, though, it's because I am totally overrun with guilt for having taken his truck the other night. I think Syke smelled something a little wrong, but he couldn't quite grasp it. I put a dollar's worth of gas in the truck before bringing it home, so the fuel level was close to where it should have been. Maybe he saw the mileage was off and then shrugged the thought away, thinking he had just remembered it wrong. I slap a smile on my face and pocket the cash, my heart pounding. *Sorry*, I think to myself. Nothing stabs at you quite like taking advantage of someone who then turns around and treats you like a princess.

Before I leave, I play three Beatle songs on my guitar, singing as loudly as I can just as my mother would.

☆

Imagine

I clutch my ticket in my hand. The letter is in the inside pocket of my jacket. I can feel it pressing against me, and it crinkles when I move.

The woman ahead of me wears a full-length coat and scarf. She rubs her hands together to warm them. Another wears a sweater underneath her jacket and thick leggings under her skirt. Her date, however, is too cool for winter clothing. Dressed in shirtsleeves, he hitches his shoulders and crosses his arms.

I send out mental vibrations to the ticket-taker who tears off my stub and the usher who points, vaguely, distantly, toward my seat: *You do not notice me. I am just anyone. Clothes. Hair. Face. When I pass, you will have forgotten me.* The mental tricks are probably a waste of energy. The Los Angeles Concert Pavilion is a huge venue. Pro basketball from fall to spring, hockey when it fits in, concerts every weekend in summer. I have memories of this place: Syke brought me here to see Heart in 1977. Dooley never lets me forget he saw Pink Floyd here once. The point is, close to twenty thousand people will step inside this building tonight, so anonymity should not be a huge problem.

I find my seat and sit up, prim and proper, with my knees together and my hands as tense as when I'm playing a really difficult guitar solo. I wish Dooley were here to hold my hand, but I'm so nervous I would probably crush his fingers. A couple in their twenties takes the two seats to my left. Right away they start making out. The two guys on my right hold monstrous Styrofoam cups, beer sloshing around inside. The one next to me wears a grayish-black ball cap, black hair sticking out from underneath like the bristles of a brush. He won't stop staring at me.

"You here all by yourself?" he asks.

I point to the couple making out. "I'm with them."

"You a big Elton John fan?"

I hear a bit of a me-Tarzan-you-Jane quality in the guy's tone. "Sure," I say. "Yes. Absolutely. Huge fan. Never miss a show."

"You know, I heard John Lennon's going to be a guest tonight."

"Really? Never liked him."

I'm saved. The lights dim. People around me begin to shriek. On stage, shadowy figures take their places behind microphones. I see guitars in silhouette, and a dark shape that must be a grand piano. A moment later I hear the opening organ arrangement to "Funeral for a Friend." People around me scream and applaud. I'm gazing into the corner, near the base of the stage.

Somewhere around here, I tell myself, I will find a door.

For a while anyway, the mission can wait. I let myself enjoy the concert. Elton John wears a gold tuxedo, a black feather boa, and eyeglasses twice the size of his head. The music is loud, and I'm close enough to feel the bass pounding against me, striking me in the chest and stomach. Usually I enjoy this feeling, the sense that the music is driving itself right into my bones, but tonight it makes me ache.

He's into his seventh song before I decide to get up from my seat and nose around.

I slip past the lovebirds and make my way up the aisle, away from the stage and toward the concession area. I meander, I blend in with the crowd, I stand in line as though I really want that two-dollar hot dog. After a few minutes, I head back into the seating area. I walk through the maze of aisles until I'm once again on the floor level. Then, when I reach the nineteenth row, where I can just see the empty spot next to the guy with bristly hair, I move past it. I send out more waves to the security people: It's not *my* seat. I sit further down *here*. I head toward the third row...the second...until I'm in a much better place for looking around. Where I now stand, maybe a hundred people have vacated their seats, choosing instead to crush against one another at the foot of the stage. Between songs, Elton John runs up and down the length of this crowd, shaking hands, signing programs, and accepting bouquets of flowers.

To my right is a curtained-off area. Behind the curtain I can just glimpse a door. I look around, step slowly away from the crowd, and move toward it. I'm just heading back to my seat is all, I tell myself. I send out vibrations of innocence. My hand touches the curtain, draws it away slightly...

"Excuse me, miss?"

"Hmm?"

A very large man steps between me and the gap in the curtain. On his belt is a small can of mace, a walkie-talkie, and a flashlight made of black metal. Over his shirt he wears a neon-yellow vest, the word *SECURITY* stenciled across it in three-inch-high letters.

"I'm afraid you're not allowed back there."

"Ohhh," I say, "I was just looking for the ladies' room."

He points into the far distance behind me, in the direction of the concession area.

"Thank you *sooo* much. I really have to go."

I head back up the aisle slowly, waiting for him to turn his head. When he does, I slip down row nineteen and back into my seat. I've found a backstage entrance. Now I just have to think of a way to get past that guard.

☆

Pepperland

At nine-fifteen, John Lennon takes the stage, and everything around me disappears. He and Elton John sing "Whatever Gets You through the Night," a hit they recorded together six years ago. I can breathe for now because he's not yet John Lennon the Beatle. Lennon sings "Stand by Me," the old Ben E. King song from the early sixties. He sings "Come Together," and my breath catches. He sings "Mother," and I sit in my seat, quietly sobbing while the guy next to me bobs and weaves in this weird little dance that has nothing to do with the song's rhythm. Lennon, as Dooley remembered, screams the chorus, and I want to scream with him. The song is about anger, about Lennon's anger that he never really had a mother. I'm angry too, so I get it. I'm in a sort of vacuum. It's just me, the man on the stage, and the music. I have just enough sense left to consider an idea: I could walk to the base of the stage, right now, and toss my mother's letter toward John Lennon. I could hurl it, Frisbee-like, so that it skims the floor of the stage and skitters to a stop at his feet. I can see the plan working in my mind—Lennon, at the end of his set, stooping to pick the letter up before he leaves. Elton John has been snagging little treasures this way all night long. I'm almost ready to try it, to head toward the base of the stage with my fingers gripping my mother's letter, when a wiser voice takes over. Lennon is not Elton John, it tells me. See how far back Lennon stands on the stage? He's less flashy than Elton, more remote. He puts distance between himself and his audience. The intimacy of the music is as much as he can bear. He's not able to make himself naked in the music and stand close to the audience too. The plan felt right a moment ago, but now when I envision it, I see the letter falling short. Lennon doesn't see it—or, not knowing what it is, ignores it. I see a custodian, alone on a dim, quiet stage, sweeping the letter away with a bunch of old rose petals and the down from a feather boa.

No. I have to give it to him. I have to put it in his hand. I have to tell him my mother's name.

Alone, with just a piano to accompany him, he sings "Imagine," and I lay my face in my hands.

Elton John performs for another hour. I get squirmy. It feels like it's time to do something, to take the next step, but the big guy in the yellow vest still stands by the curtain. I can feel a shift, though, in the evening's energy. Elton is in a second encore. A few people in the crowd filter toward the exits, hoping to beat the traffic out of the parking lot. The beer drinker in the seat next to me yawns.

As I watch, a short line of people forms near the curtain. Most are Syke's age or older, and they all wear a little badge pinned to the front of their jackets. One by one they file past the security guard, who glances at each badge and nods. A tingling inside my chest lifts me from my seat and starts me walking toward them. *Slowly,* I tell myself. *With confidence. Like you belong with the group. Like anyone can see you have a right to be with them, a right to step backstage and visit your old friend John Lennon.* The tingling inside me grows until I realize what it is: I'm terrified. The voice that only a moment ago told me to walk with confidence now screams at me. *You have no badge, Star.*

I join the group and try to make myself as invisible as possible. Ahead of me is a very fat man with shaggy hair, wispy beard, and a huge camera dangling from a strap around his neck. While the guard checks the man's badge, I slip around toward the open door.

"Excuse me, miss. *Miss!* Would you stop right there please?" The voice is like a hand clamping down on my shoulder.

"Hmm?"

"May I see your badge?"

I pat the front of my jacket, the rear pockets of my jeans. "Sorry," I say. "Left it in my purse. Be right back."

I return to my seat, fuming.

As time passes, the crowd thickens at the backstage door. I can guess who they are. They're magazine and newspaper reporters. They're local VIPs. They're people who were lucky enough, at contest time, to be the ninth caller to the radio station. Two guards now stand at the curtain, shining flashlights on those stupid green passes. They stop everyone. They look at faces. I have to act soon, I tell myself. I'm here. I'm ready. I am on a mission. I'm doing this for my mom. I sense I only have a few moments, and I know I have to make a decision. If I'm going, I have to go *now*. Briefly I think about consequences. I imagine handcuffs and surly policemen, and the thought makes me pause.

The crowd grows smaller. When they're gone, I'll have no chance at all. I push myself from my seat and head back toward the doorway and the line of people with passes.

Then I see it. The security guards have made a mistake. The people, impatient to get backstage, have crowded together, and the guards haven't forced them back into single file. Three or four flash their badges at once. Everyone's talking. The music is loud, pulsing. I come up behind the group, wait for a moment when several are pressing themselves on the guards, and I slip around them. The move isn't perfect. Behind me I hear one guard talking to the other. "Did you see someone go in?" A second later the same voice grows louder, calling to me. "Miss! Hey, you!"

The hallway takes a sharp turn. When I'm beyond it, I speed up.

I brush past those ahead of me, keeping their bodies

between the security guards and me. I tell myself the guards won't come after me right away. Too many people are waiting, too many badges to check and faces to note. I tell myself the man wasn't even sure I'd slipped in. I was just a bit of motion and color; I could have been anything—someone's jacket flapping, an impatient reporter shifting around the edge of the group. I take a deep breath and try not to move quite so fast. I no longer hear the voice of the security guard calling. The footsteps behind me are slow and unhurried.

The area below and behind the stage appears to be used for maintenance. The walls are solid concrete; the floor is concrete with a rubber mat. Our footsteps make a rubbery echo. We're in a maze of tunnels. Above my head are weak fluorescent tubes that glow an amber color, turning everything a muddy yellow. I stay close to the wall and away from other people. They chat as if they all know one another. Just ahead is the shaggy-haired man with the camera. Popping open the back, he slips in a fresh roll of film, closes the camera, then sucks on his forefinger as though he snagged it in the clasp.

We take several turns—rights, lefts; I can't keep track of them all. We finally arrive at the end of a long hallway. I see a door, maybe sixty feet away, and I have to stop and lean against the wall a moment. The door is *right there.* On the other side of the door is a room, and I tell myself I know who's in the room. I know what I'll do when I get inside. I don't have the words yet, but I'm starting to hear them in my head. *Mr. Lennon, my name is Star...*

Several people file past me. My hand reaches to the pocket of my jacket, presses down, and I hear my mother's letter crinkle. No more turns. No more mad dashes. I've made it. I'm about to meet John Lennon, and I just have to breathe. Just breathe and take a few more steps.

I move forward with the crowd. The door opens, and the

first few people wearing their little badges step inside. I hear laughter and shouts of greeting. Behind me, I hear scuffling, but I don't think much about it. I'm looking at the open door. I reach into my pocket and remove the letter, clasping it in both hands.

"Excuse me—excuse me," shouts a voice. "Stop right there."

I turn, and four security guards surround me. I don't recognize any of them. They've never seen me. How did they...?

One reaches for the walkie-talkie on his belt. "Team leader," he says, "Area Nine is secure. We've got her."

"What's your name?"

"Pamela Cochran. It's on the driver's license you're holding."

They've taken me to a security area, a room not much larger than my bedroom at home. Eight or ten guys in yellow vests hang around, mostly sipping coffee and ignoring me. I feel a little jab of anger, like a sliver under a fingernail, when I notice that the entire security crew is male. Then I smile. I must be channeling Mom. A moment ago one of the guards shoved a folding steel chair in my direction and told me to sit. I did. Instantly. The guy didn't sound like he wanted to have a discussion about it. Now a man in a suit—the head of security, I figure—stands over me. He studies my license photo, then my face, then my photo again.

"Do I get a lawyer and a phone call?" I ask.

"You might not want to get too smart with me," he says. "I have a lot of leeway as to how I handle this, and I'll tell you up front your attitude will have a whole lot to do with the choices I make. Here, you can put this away."

Imagine

He hands my license back to me. I decide to take his advice and keep my mouth shut. In front of me is a console with twelve separate television screens, each one black-and-white and no more than five inches square. On one screen I see tech people removing microphones and guitar stands from the stage, coiling up lengths of cable and wheeling off a grand piano. The other screens carry essentially the same message. Each one shows, from every possible angle, the end of an event: empty seats, cleaning crews with push brooms and plastic trash bags, stragglers heading toward exits. The night is over.

And I've failed.

"Good job, people," shouts the man in the suit.

I recognize one of the guards. He's the one who sent me off to the restroom, the one I slipped by only minutes later. He walks over and stands above me now, arms folded and eyes glaring. "What do you want to do with her?" he asks.

The head of security is a tall man with dark hair, which he slicks back in straight, feathery lines. An old scar runs from the corner of his mouth to the tip of his chin, giving his face a wrinkled, cowboy look. "You're lucky," he says to me. "I could hand you over to the police for trespassing."

"But you won't?"

"Miss, you lucked out. Tonight we busted two guys for hawking bootleg tour sweatshirts, we called an ambulance for a pregnant lady who went into early labor, and we caught a kid selling joints out of a stall in the boys' john. I'm tired, I'm cranky, and I want to go home. So an overanxious groupie, frankly, is a waste of my time." He looks at the other guard. "Walk her out. Follow her all the way to the lobby doors."

The guard says nothing to me as we leave. His walkie-talkie crackles, and he twists a knob on it, clicking it off. Now, except for a few thin, scattered noises, the arena is silent. Our footsteps tap lightly on the floor. Someone three levels away laughs, and the sound is so tiny it could be a child's laugh. The arena is a great empty space. It seemed smaller when I came in. When it was filled with people, the paths from level to level were shorter, the rows of seats fewer, the stage closer. Now the place seems to go on forever. The walk out is all uphill. My legs ache.

The guard pushes open the lobby door and waits for me to step past him. I say thank you, and he actually smiles. "Win some, lose some," he says. Then, to cheer me up, he tries to be helpful. "Come back when AC/DC is playing. Those guys'll let anybody in."

"I'll keep that in mind," I say.

The parking lot has grown larger too. I see a few last cars lined at the nearest gate—and a wide river of red taillights heading down the road toward the freeway—but mostly I just see acres and acres of empty blacktop. Syke's dented tan pickup sits nearly a quarter of a mile away, alone between two yellow parking stripes. It looks tiny, like a toy, and I can't imagine I'll ever get to it walking. The air around me feels thick. As a child, when I went to the neighborhood pool, I would sometimes blow all the air out of my body and let myself sink to the bottom. I could walk along the floor of the deep end, just a few steps, before I would have to come up again for air. That's how I feel right now—like I'm moving in slow motion, walking through water.

When I reach the truck, I fumble with the keys, struggle to find the hole in the lock. Finally the door opens, and I step into the cab. The sense of weariness I feel is almost overwhelming. I place my hands on the steering wheel, but a moment later they slip off and fall into my lap. My head tips back. My eyes close.

I want to cry. I want to be hysterical. I'd like to feel that familiar tingle that tells me that my old anger is about to hit me like a wave. I can see myself pounding the seats with my fists, but I don't have the energy. I do nothing. I've failed—I've failed myself and my mother—and crying and pounding the seats won't give me another chance.

I'm so *tired.*

I'm drifting. Weird memories float in and out of my mind. I remember a time when I slipped on my roller skates and skinned my leg. I feel the sting, see the red scraped skin stretching from my knee to my ankle. I remember a time when another girl teased me at school because my front tooth had fallen out and landed in my lap. I remember having chicken pox, the itchy bumps covering my back, chest, arms, and the soothing pink lotion that cooled my skin. I remember seventh grade, when Toby Atherton kissed me on the lips, then said "Yuck!" I remember one year at summer camp, when my leg swelled from a spider bite that looked like two tiny red eyes staring out from a round face of bruised skin. As these thoughts pass, part of me watches and looks for a thread, something that ties them together. I struggle for a while, but then I finally understand: I wanted my mother. In every case, I wanted her to put her arms around me, to find the right words to comfort me. Mostly, I wanted her to make it all go away. That's what I want right now. I want it all to go away— the anger that always seems to be churning inside my stomach, the slamming door in my head that keeps me from writing a song, the knowledge that John Lennon was a few feet away and I couldn't reach him. I want arms around me, a cheek pressed against my head, a voice whispering in my ear making everything better. I want my mom.

I know her voice, her face, her spirit so well, I can imagine her sitting next to me. I know exactly how she'd reach over and take my hand, or how she might lay her palm against the side of my face and draw my head to her shoulder. Now, in my mind, I can feel her doing just that. My forehead rests comfortably in the hollow of her neck. Her hand stays on my cheek. I can feel her rocking me back and forth. *It's okay,* she says. And as she says those same words over and over, they begin to take on the rhythm of our rocking.

It's okay...it's okay...

17

(Just Like) Starting Over

So you never got to meet him," says Dr. Artaud.

"I never did."

"And how do you feel?"

"About not meeting John Lennon?" I ask.

"About anything—everything."

I have to ponder awhile before I can answer this question. I had spent the last month or so thinking about John Lennon. In my mind the meeting had occurred dozens of different ways. Sometimes we would shake hands; sometimes we wouldn't. Sometimes I would talk about my mother in a long gush; other times I would only mention her name, tell Mr. Lennon how she loved his music, and leave off with the fact she had died. In those fantasies, Lennon would take over from there, making me laugh at a funny story about Julia or his aunt Mimi. Sometimes I imagined a group of security guards knocking sheepishly on the door of the backstage green room. "Sorry, Mr. Lennon," one would say. "We shouldn't have let her get past us. We'll escort her out immediately." Lennon, in reply, would wave them off. "Let her stay," he would tell them. "We're having a lovely chat." The scenes went on and on, playing out differently each time, but in all of them I met John

Lennon. I told him about my mother. I gave him the letter. Now, days after the concert, days after I failed, after none of my fantasies came true, I should be unhappy. The old anger should be bouncing around inside me, taking shots at me like I'm the target kid in a game of dodge ball. I should be throwing something, knocking a chair over—but I'm not. I don't feel that way anymore.

Dr. Artaud interrupts my thoughts. "Star?"

"Yeah?"

"Did you hear my question?"

"Yeah…yeah."

I think about Teri and what she taught me about songwriting, how a song comes alive in the details. I should make a picture for Dr. Artaud with words so that, whatever I feel, she can feel it with me. "When I was five," I begin, "my mother took me to the beach. I was playing in the surf, and I remember how the waves would slap against me, and how the water would seem to grab at my legs when it pulled back. It was a little scary, but I knew my mom was standing a few feet behind me, so I was completely safe. If I went out too far, or if I fell, she would grab me and haul me back."

"Okay."

I shrug as if the rest of the answer is obvious. "Well…that's how I feel."

Dr. Artaud starts to write something down, pauses, fiddles with her pen, then sets everything—pen and pad, the file folder with my name on it—down on her desk. Her hand reaches over and clicks off the little cassette recorder she uses to tape some of our sessions. Smiling, she leans back in her chair.

"What's next?" she asks.

"I have an idea," I tell her, but I'm not ready to say anything more.

(Just Like) Starting Over

☆

I figure it comes down to this: The sun low in the sky, the beach in front of me, my mom's guitar over my left shoulder, and her letter to John Lennon in my back pocket. They're like four compass points. No matter what direction I turn, I'm facing one of them. I lean the guitar against the chain-link fence and yank off my sneakers. The sand is cold between my toes, and I feel goose bumps prickling up and down my shins.

"Wait here, okay?" I ask.

Dooley stands behind me. He nods and plops himself in the sand. His long legs fold under him, and his back rests against the metal fencepost. "I'm good," he says.

I point to the art pad under his arm. "Show me again."

He tears a sheet of paper from the pad and slowly creases it down the middle. He folds one corner back, then another. I watch, nodding as I follow each fold, each pinch. The sheet of paper, over the next three or four minutes, takes on a new shape.

"Got it?" he asks.

I bite my lip. "Think so."

Today the Pacific is the color of the chalkboards at school—almost black. It looks hard, too. I have this odd thought that if you could freeze its motion, the ripples could cut you. The sky is slate gray, and clouds are floating between me and the sun, which is low in the sky and orange. It makes the edges of the clouds look as though they're on fire. The day is breezy. The wind comes from behind me and kicks my hair up in streams.

I reach for my guitar and start across the sand. A few seagulls circle around cawing, but otherwise the beach is empty. A large wave crashes against the shore, and a moment later I feel a mist of salt spray tickle my face. I wipe my hand across my cheeks and smile. The lifeguard stand is thirty yards away, a little white shack on four stilts. The number twelve, stenciled on the side in bright red paint, looks purple in the gray light. I walk closer, pausing at the bottom of it. The guitar digs into my shoulder, so I shift it around a bit. I'll have to climb the rungs using one hand.

When I reach the top, I set the guitar down and draw my mother's letter from my back pocket. It's wrinkled and a little damp, but in one piece. Once again, seeing her name, her handwriting, catches me and takes my breath away. I stare at it for a very long time, then squeeze my eyes tightly shut. My thumb digs below the flap and lodges there, waiting. "One..." I say, "two..." I never get to three. My thumb rips across the flap and tears the envelope open. When I look down, I see a sheet of pastel-colored stationery peeking out from the opening.

I smile and sniffle a little. I remember the notes my mother used to leave for me. They were always full of scratched-out words and crowded letters and little notations in the margins. The lines in her notes always angled upward as she wrote them. I read one time that was a sign of a happy person. So I'm a little surprised to see that her letter to John Lennon is perfect. The margins are straight; I see no smears of ink, no Xs through words, no hurried slash marks dotting her *I*s. I can picture her in my mind, pouring out this letter again and again on sheets of notebook paper, crossing out entire paragraphs, editing every phrase until it was perfect. She's like me when I'm writing a song. I wonder how many pieces of stationery she wasted copying the letter over, crumpling one every time she misspelled a word or crowded a line. And I'm laughing as I read. The letter is silly and childish and so beautiful it hurts.

(Just Like) Starting Over

She screamed while watching the Beatles on Ed Sullivan. She did a study of the harmony in "I Want to Hold Your Hand" for a college music class, and received an A from the professor. She wrote a poem for Lennon then threw it away because she was too embarrassed to send it. As I'm reading, I can hear my mother's voice, the rhythms of her speech, but the voice is a higher pitch. I can't think of another way to explain it. I hear a girl talking.

Laughing, crying, I take the sheet and crease it down the middle. Then I take one of the corners and fold it back as well. I remember what Dooley showed me, eye the creases carefully and keep them sharp. Two more folds, and one end of the stiff paper comes to an arrow point. Another fold, then another, and I've created a weighted line down the center. The front bends down a little now. I pinch. I sculpt. I'm not an expert like Dooley, but to my eye the final shape is perfect. It balances well in my hand. It feels right.

I stand up and hold my breath.

The sun peeks out from the clouds, sending down a stream of light between them. I aim for that. Drawing my arm back, I let the air out of my lungs at the same instant I let go of the letter. It has a nose now, and wings, and the breeze catches it and hurls it into the sky. It rises. A seagull darts from its path.

I watch as the letter soars out over the water. Another gust of wind hits it, sending it even higher. A moment later it dips, curves, then banks just as a new wave is forming in the surf. It gets smaller and smaller, until it's a dot of pink against the bright orange of the sunset. Then even the little dot disappears.

I never see it land.

I sit down now, reaching for my guitar and hugging it to me. I play a little to get the feel of it and to loosen the cold from my fingers. I strum a simple A chord, then I mess with it. It becomes an A9, which sounds richer and more…unresolved. A ninth chord sounds like it's not sure where it wants to go, and I like that. The chord suggests a lick, and my fingers find it. I play it again, then a third time, because it tickles my ears. A word comes to mind: *Soaring.* The word makes me think of the seagulls and the clouds and the sun and the sheet of paper I turned into a bird. I smile. My fingers find another lick.

You picked me up, held me above your head
I spread my arms, and I was flying…

The words come by themselves. I don't look for them. I feel my way through a chord change, and more words follow. I sing them, my ear finding a melody that suits the harmonies I'm building on the fingerboard. More folk than blues, I tell myself. And sweet.

Another set of images comes to me: the warmth of the sun on my shoulders, the wind kicking my hair—and the paper airplane, the idea of something beneath me lifting me up.

The images start to assemble themselves into something.

Dooley is still waiting for me when I finish. He's sitting where I left him, only now a lamppost throws a cone of light down over his shoulders, and his shape casts a long shadow across the asphalt. He stands when he sees me coming. It's not until I step into the light that he notices I'm crying. I'm gripping my guitar, and I'm crying and laughing at the same time. I can't stop.

"What's—?"

Before he can finish, I place my hand behind his neck and draw him to me. My mouth touches his. It's a long, clumsy, teeth-clicking sort of kiss, and it's wonderful. When we pull away, I start laughing again, and I press my wet face into his shirt. I'm shaking, and I can feel his arms slowly slip around me.

Finally, after several moments, I look up at him. He wipes his thumbs across the wetness on my cheeks, and I sniffle.

"Hey," I ask, "wanna hear a song I wrote for my mom?"

Afterword

Getting It Wrong
to Get It Right

It takes a certain amount of—call it nerve, chutzpah, hubris—to write a novel that fictionalizes an icon. John Lennon doesn't actually appear in *Pepperland*. He's a force, a presence who fills gaps in the novel the way air fills even tiny spaces in a room. When writing about someone so well known, an author has a duty to be as accurate as possible and to get the history exactly right. But authors also have another duty—to write a good story. History gives us events in the order in which they happen, and it doesn't much care whether those events follow the arc of a novel. Writers hate that.

So I confess. I lied.

I took care to be accurate about the historical details in the narrative, but in one instance, I changed history.

Pepperland begins in the fall of 1980. Star tries to meet John Lennon by sneaking backstage during a concert Lennon shares with Elton John. These two men did not perform live together in 1980.

The truth is, Lennon made a guest appearance at an Elton John concert in 1974. It turned out to be his last public performance.

In late 1980, Lennon released what would be his final album—*Double Fantasy*. The new songs fired up fans' imaginations. Some people believed the Beatles might perform together again. Real dreamers envisioned a reunion tour. Lennon himself, who over the years seemed least interested in re-forming the band, considered it a possibility.

It never happened.

On December 8, 1980, a week or so after the events of *Pepperland*, a young man named Mark David Chapman accosted Lennon as the singer left his apartment building. Chapman handed Lennon a copy of the new record and asked for an autograph. Lennon signed the album and went off to a recording session, seeing the moment as nothing more than a casual meeting between an artist and a fan. Hours later Lennon and his wife, Yoko, returned. In the dark hallway of their apartment building, a voice called Lennon's name. Lennon paused. Someone standing in the shadows then stepped forward and fired three gunshots. A security guard heard the shots and wrestled the shooter to the ground. It was Chapman, the man who had only hours ago asked Lennon for an autograph.

"Do you know what you've done?" the guard shouted.

"Yes," said Chapman. "I just killed John Lennon."

So why did I lie? Star's story needed John Lennon. Lennon was a living bridge connecting Star to her mother. And that's the truth I cared about most.